THE NEON LAWYER

Other titles by Victor Methos

Jon Stanton Thrillers

White Angel Murder
Walk in Darkness
Sin City Homicide
Arsonist
The Porn Star Murders
Sociopath
Black Widow
Run Away

Mickey Parsons Thrillers

The Murder of Janessa Hennley
The Bastille

Sarah King Mysteries

Blood Dahlia

Plague Trilogy Medical Thrillers

Plague
Pestilence
Scourge

Stand-Alone Thrillers

Titanoboa
The Extinct
Sea Creature
Superhero
Serial Murder and Other Neat Tricks
Murder Corporation
Diary of an Assassin
Black Sky
Dracula–A Modern Telling
Savage
Earl Lindquist: Accountant and Zombie Killer

Science Fiction & Fantasy

Clone Hunter
Empire of War
Blood Rain
Star Dreamer: The Early Short Fiction of Victor Methos
Black Onyx
Black Onyx Reloaded
The Vampire Diaries: The Beautiful

THE
NEON
LAWYER

VICTOR METHOS

THOMAS & MERCER

Published by Thomas & Mercer, Seattle

www.apub.com

Amazon, the Amazon logo, and Thomas & Mercer are trademarks of Amazon.com, Inc., or its affiliates.

ISBN-13: 9781477825976
ISBN-10: 1477825975

Cover design by Damonza.com

Library of Congress Control Number: 2014940481

Printed in the United States of America

For Sam, Noah, Jonah, and Linds. The stars in my sky.

At his best, man is the noblest of animals.
Separated from law and justice, he is the worst.

—Aristotle

Based on a True Story

One

The young girl saw the candy the man was holding.

A blue van was behind him with the sliding door open, and the man flashed a wide smile. The girl had seen him before. He'd come to her school and sat across the street in his van. He had waved to her once but she hadn't waved back. Her mother had taught her not to talk to people she didn't know.

"I'm not supposed to talk to strangers."

"Well, that's great, sweetheart," he said, the smile still in place. "That's a good lesson. But my name is Ty. What's yours?"

"Tabitha."

"Tabitha. That's such a pretty name. And you're six years old, I bet." She nodded. "Yeah, I'm six."

"Well, Tabitha, I'm forty-two. See? Now we're not strangers anymore. You know me and I know you. Take the candy. It's fine. I have some balloons here, too."

She had seen the balloons earlier and was wondering about them. They were different colors: green, blue, red, purple, and pink. Pink was her favorite color, and she was going to ask for one of those, but thought she should ask her mother first. Her mother had told her that no one ever gave anything away for nothing—that if something seemed too good to be true, then it probably was. Tabitha was pretty sure that meant she would have to pay for the balloon.

"Do you want a balloon, sweetheart?"

She nodded. "But I don't have any money."

The man chuckled. "It's free, darling. Just because you're so pretty. Now which one would you like?"

"A pink one."

"A pink one? Well, that's a great choice. Let me get it for you."

The man climbed into the van and untangled a pink balloon from the others. He crawled to the open door and held the balloon out to her. His hands were dirty, and she could see black underneath his fingernails. "Here ya go."

Tabitha smiled and took a few steps forward. When she reached out and grabbed the string of the balloon, she felt pressure on her arm. It hurt, and she didn't know what it was, but then she saw the man's hand. His fingers were turning white because he was squeezing her arm so tightly.

His face had changed. He had been smiling before, but now his face looked like something she saw in her bedroom at night whenever her night-light went out, something that would give her nightmares. Even his eyes looked different. She was so scared she couldn't even scream.

"I have more presents for you in here," the man growled.

He hauled her into the van and slammed the sliding door shut.

Two

Brigham Theodore leapt over a pothole. He dashed across the sidewalk as if in a race, but there were no competitors. A homeless man sat slumped against one of the buildings. Brigham sprinted past him, then stopped and turned around. He had several dollars he was saving for a celebratory lunch. Brigham kept two dollars for himself and gave the rest to the homeless man, who said, "God bless," with a wide smile.

"No problem," Brigham said, before he started his sprint again.

An intersection light turned red and he glanced both ways before dashing across. A white cargo truck blared its horn and swerved around him.

Brigham didn't know how he'd missed such a large vehicle barreling toward him. He waved and shouted, "Sorry!" but kept going.

The convention center was packed. Over two hundred newly minted lawyers were being sworn in that day. The Salt Lake City swearing-in was always held in the Salt Palace. Brigham hoped there would be snacks because he hadn't eaten yet, having rushed to the convention center straight from work.

The principal of the elementary school where he worked as a "facilities technician"—the new fancy term for janitor—had allowed him this morning off, but he had to be back before afternoon. He was fairly certain he would be the first member of the Bar in Utah to also be a janitor.

Brigham rushed across the street. The building had been remodeled recently but it still looked like the basketball arena it used to be. Several posters were up for Salt Lake Comic Con, which had taken place almost three months ago.

He took the stairs two at a time, ran through some doors and up another set of stairs. In a large auditorium, two hundred people in suits milled around as family members sat on folding chairs and snapped photos with their phones.

Brigham slipped into the group. Almost everyone there knew each other since they'd gone to the University of Utah or Brigham Young University. But he was a transplant from Tulane. After Hurricane Katrina, his law school class had been cancelled. Rather than transferring, he took some time off, then came back later and finished. He'd wanted to practice somewhere rural. Most big cities had a lawyer for every six or seven people. The markets were so saturated that no one could find a job. And the jobs that were available either didn't pay much or expected you to live at the firm. He wanted neither, so he'd picked the place that looked just about as far from New Orleans as he could get: Salt Lake City, Utah.

"Ladies and gentlemen, please take your seats," someone announced.

More folding chairs had been set up for the admittees. Brigham sat at the end of a row next to a man with an unlit cigar in his mouth. The chief justice of the Utah Supreme Court spoke for a few minutes about the grandeur and importance of the law, and about how she reminded her husband, who was a physician, that while his professional forebears were bleeding people with leeches two hundred years ago, hers were drafting the constitution of the United States. The story got a laugh.

Then the dean of the University of Utah spoke about the grand ol' profession and told some anecdotes about the one year he actually practiced law before joining academia.

The chief justice took the podium again and asked the admittees to stand. Brigham got to his feet with the others. The chief justice administered the oath, stating each sentence and waiting as the admittees repeated it:

I am fully subject to the laws of the state of Utah and the laws of the United States and will abide by the same.

I will support the constitution of the state of Utah and the Constitution of the United States.

I will abide by the Rules of Professional Conduct approved by the Supreme Court of the State of Utah.

I will maintain the respect due to the courts of justice and judicial officers.

I will not counsel or maintain any suit or proceeding which shall appear to me to be unjust or any defense except as I believe to be honestly debatable under the law, unless it is in defense of a person charged with a public offense. I will employ for the purpose of maintaining the causes confided to me only those means consistent with truth and honor. I will never seek to mislead the judge or jury by any artifice or false statement.

I will maintain the confidence and preserve inviolate the secrets of my client, and will accept no compensation in connection with the business of my client unless this compensation is from or with the knowledge and approval of the client or with the approval of the court.

I will abstain from all offensive personalities, and advance no fact prejudicial to the honor or reputation of a party or witness unless required by the justice of the cause with which I am charged.

I will never reject, from any consideration personal to myself, the cause of the defenseless or oppressed, or delay unjustly the cause of any person.

Brigham repeated the words, excited and nervous and frightened all at once. When the oath was done, cheers went up from the crowd behind him as they clapped for their loved ones. No one was there for him, so he left after he received his certificates.

A hot dog vendor was around the corner, and Brigham bought one with everything on it. Sitting down at the curb, he ate and stared at his certificates. He kept re-reading his Bar certificate: the title of the court with his name underneath stating that he was authorized to practice law. He could now give advice and get money for it in exchange. A smile came to his lips, but it only lasted a moment. He had to be back at the school and in uniform.

He finished his hot dog and began the quick walk back to the school, his certificates tucked under his arm.

Three

Amanda Pierce sat in her car and felt the ridges of the gun. The handle, the muzzle, the weight of it. Everyone in Utah carried guns, most of them openly in holsters, but she'd never seen the need. Salt Lake City, by national standards, was a safe place. What crime there was consisted primarily of DUIs and pot charges.

The two deputies were walking down the stairs of the courthouse with a man between them. He looked almost normal, other than the orange jumpsuit that read UTAH DOC across the back and up the side of his leg. The handcuffs were tight around his wrists. He was a large man, both fat and muscle-bound, and at least six foot two. He appeared grizzled and had a tattoo on his neck that looked like the remnant of some disease.

Amanda looked down at the gun. She closed her eyes a moment. Opening them, she looked at the photograph that hung from her rearview mirror: a six-year-old girl in a Halloween costume, a princess with a wand and sparkling pink shoes.

Tears flowed down Amanda's cheeks. She sobbed, unable to hold them back. The emotion tightened her throat, and she felt as if she couldn't breathe. She wept like that several times a day. At first she'd fought the tears, trying to put on a brave face. But she wasn't fooling anyone, least of all herself. She was broken in a way that could never be repaired, that could never be made whole. And whenever she wasn't fully occupied, the tears came.

She looked at the man again. He was laughing at something one of the deputies had said.

She tucked the gun in her purse and got out of her car. The crutch in the backseat was worn out, and the rubber stop on the bottom was peeling. Every time she saw it, it took her right back to Kandahar Province and the landmine that had taken her leg off below the knee. She hesitated, then tucked the crutch under her arm and turned toward the courthouse.

The sky was gray but sunny. Salt Lake City had some of the worst air pollution in the United States. Several successive governors had allowed big business to release whatever they wanted in the air. And since the valley was in a bowl surrounded by mountains, none of the pollution ever really left. Amanda found it fitting that the sky itself would be sick today.

Keeping her head low, she walked across the lawn of the courthouse. A van from the Salt Lake County Metro Jail was parked there with a deputy in the driver's seat, waiting for the prisoner. Amanda crossed in front of the prisoner and the two deputies. She climbed a few steps. When they were farther away from her, she stopped and turned around.

Amanda's gun came out quickly. She had imagined the moment every second of every day for the past week. And each time she'd envisioned it, the scene had been in slow motion. She'd thought it would take longer to get the gun out, giving her time to think. She'd thought the deputies transporting the prisoner would have time to react, and the prisoner would see what was coming. She needed him to see and to know it was her.

She raised the gun. "Hey!"

The man and the deputies turned. Their faces showed disbelief, and one of the deputies reached for his gun.

"This is for Tabitha," she said.

The trigger gave easily. The man's mouth was open and he could only get out the beginnings of a word as the first round tore into him. The second and third missed, going wide, but the rest hit him. They ripped through his head and he flew off his feet, tumbling down the courthouse steps.

The deputy had his gun out, but Amanda dropped her weapon and held up her hands. She was smiling as tears ran down her cheeks, still smiling as the deputy tackled her and as the cold steel of the handcuffs closed around her wrists.

Four

Brigham worked until six in the evening, finishing with a final round of the halls to make sure he hadn't missed anything. As he walked by the teachers' lounge, he saw his boss, Rick, with his feet up on the couch, sipping a beer. Rick's skin was a light black, but his hair was pure gray, almost white. No one that Brigham ever knew could accurately guess his age. Their eyes met and Rick smiled.

"Come in here, B."

Brigham walked in and collapsed into a chair. Every muscle felt tight, and his feet were sore, but the exhilaration of the swearing-in ceremony hadn't faded. He still felt giddy, like he could go dancing or to a party and have a good time, but he had neither the money nor the friends for either.

"How come you never go out?" Rick asked.

"Don't really know anyone."

"You been here over a year. Maybe it's time."

Brigham leaned back into the soft recliner. "The only people I get to see every day are you guys."

He chuckled. "Yeah, we ain't the most social group. But you're a young kid. What're you, twenty-six?"

"Yeah."

"You should be out bangin' every chick in sight. Whatchyoo doin' mopping floors with me?"

"Money's money."

He shook his head. "Not for you. You don't belong here, B. I've seen how smart you are. Them books you read on your breaks, I can't even understand 'em. You still in school, right?"

"I'm done. I just got sworn into the Bar today."

"The Bar?"

"Yeah, I'm officially a lawyer."

Rick was silent a moment and then burst out laughing. "Well, you the only lawyer I seen workin' a mop." He rose and went to the mini-fridge, took out another beer that was hidden in a plastic bag underneath some vegetables, and handed it to Brigham. "Congrats. Seriously."

They tapped bottles, and Brigham took a long drink. The beer stung going down and was cold.

"So, what now?" Rick asked as he kicked his feet up again.

"I gotta get a job."

"Lotta jobs?"

Brigham took a drink and shook his head. "Nope. But I'm gonna take my résumé to every law firm I can find and see what happens."

"Well, that's good. My granddaddy was a lawyer. I ever tell you that?"

"No."

"Yup. Civil rights lawyer down south in Mississippi during all the bullshit when that was goin' down. They killed him for it, man. He was walkin' out of a grocery store one night and *pop*. They shot him in the head. One shot. Killed him 'cause he didn't think black folk should be beaten by the police. I remember him, though. He used to tell me that the Good Lord always lets justice win in the end, that's what he'd say. 'Good Lord'll let justice always win in the end.' I remember that much about him, but them boys that killed him got arrested and then acquitted by a white Mississippi jury." He zoned out a moment, his eyes glazing over as he stared at a spot on the wall. "Don't see how justice won, there."

Brigham thought back to his own grandfather, a convicted felon and con man. Brigham remembered the smell of the jails when he'd visit his grandfather—sweat and Lysol. The only thing his grandfather had ever taught him was how to put electrical tape on a dollar bill and feed it into a vending machine, then pull it out at the last second: buy a soda, and keep the change.

"Was your dad a lawyer too?" Brigham asked.

"Nah, he didn't have the head for it. Me neither. My daddy was a car mechanic and I ended up out here, man. But I ain't complainin'. I put in a good twenty and my retirement is set. I can leave any time."

"Why don't you?"

"Since Mandy died, I don't wanna be alone. Sandwiches and TV is all I got waitin' for me at home." He finished his beer and rose with a groan, placing the bottle back in the plastic bag to be taken home. "You take tomorrow off, and go find yourself a job, you hear?"

"I will. Thanks, Rick."

Rick placed his hand on Brigham's shoulder as he left. Brigham waited a few minutes, then finished the beer and headed home. He would have a long day tomorrow.

⌣

Home was nothing more than a studio apartment in an area of the city known as the Avenues. The streets were so narrow and the stop signs so confusing that he could never see which direction cars were coming from. Traffic lights seemed to be placed at random, and every day or two, Brigham would hear the metallic crunch of an accident.

He rode his bicycle up the streets toward an old Victorian house. It had been split into five apartments and he rented the basement—the cheapest space. His apartment was down a hallway and a set of winding, dilapidated stairs. As he rolled his bike inside, one of the other tenants in the house opened her door.

June was dressed in a black Depeche Mode T-shirt and black jeans, with a white beanie on her head. Her glasses were thin and warped and looked like they might fall off her head any second.

"Hey," she said.

"Hey."

"Working late?"

"Had to take a couple of hours off today, so I stayed late to make up for it." He hesitated, but had to tell her. The pressure was building up inside him, and he might explode if he didn't. "I got sworn in to the Bar today."

"No way! I thought that was, like, next year."

"No, it was today."

She hugged him, and he could smell her body wash.

"Seriously, congratulations, Brigham. You going out to celebrate?"

"Um, no. I thought I'd just hang out."

"What? No way. We're going out."

"You don't have to, June."

"Bullshit. We're going."

"Lemme change, then."

⌣

Brigham took a quick shower and changed into jeans and a button-down shirt. June was sitting on his couch watching television. She rose and fixed his collar. June had been fixing his collar since he'd moved into the complex. They would hang out, watch *Battlestar Galactica* together on Netflix, and go out for dinner sometimes when neither of them had plans. Never had it gone past that. She was literally his only friend right now, and sex had a way of ruining friendships. The cost wasn't worth the benefit.

They walked to a nearby barbecue restaurant as the sun set. It was right next to a vegan restaurant, and legend had it that the owners had once gotten into a fistfight.

Several people were walking dogs, and a few joggers were out, too. The Avenues wasn't a place to raise a family, so instead there were couples with dogs.

The waitress seated them at the window next to some football players from the university, and June ordered bruschetta. The restaurant was always packed with the college crowd, and the football players already had several empty beer bottles on their table. They were loud enough that the waitress asked them if they could quiet down.

"So what now, Brigham? Conquering the world one case at a time?"

"I don't know about that. There's no jobs. You got two law schools here pumping out lawyers in a state that doesn't need any more. It's the same story nationwide. It's a dying profession, I think."

"There'll always be lawyers. People can't settle arguments by themselves. Besides, all the politicians are lawyers—they're not going to let the profession disappear."

"Maybe." He tried some of the bruschetta. It was so oily that it dripped onto his shirt, and he dabbed at it with a napkin. "What about you? That art degree's gotta come in handy somewhere."

"I think the people who major in dance have better prospects than art majors. I may have to—"

"Hey!" one of the men at the next table shouted. "Hey, boo, what's your name?"

Brigham glanced over. The men were eyeballing June as if she were sitting at the table by herself.

"Ignore them," she said.

"Hey, boo, come over here. Have a drink with us. Don't be all shy."

Brigham turned to them. "She's with me, fellas. We're good."

"Hey, fuck you, queer. We ain't talkin' to you."

16

Whenever Brigham's father was drunk, he would get the belt and take out his aggression on Brigham or Brigham's mother. When he sobered up, he would cry and beg their forgiveness. Everything would be fine, until the next time he got drunk. Drunk bravado had a special place in Brigham's heart.

Brigham felt his anger rising, but told himself that when people drank, they weren't themselves. The college students were just drunk.

"How about next round's on me, fellas?"

"How about I fuck that skinny bitch in the ass and make you watch, yo."

Brigham smiled and turned away. He had a glass of water in front of him, and next to that was the plate of bruschetta.

"Brigham, ignore them."

He grabbed the plate, twisted around, and hurled it as hard as he could. It slammed into the football player's face, tomatoes slopping down onto his collar.

"Time to go," Brigham said, grabbing June's arm and pulling her out of the restaurant.

The three players were on their feet, so drunk that they nearly fell over each other. But even drunk, they were faster and stronger than Brigham. He turned the corner into an alley between the vegan restaurant and the barbecue place, still clinging to June's arm, and made a dash for the street.

The players were too fast and they were already on him, grabbing his arms from behind. One of them circled around—the one with the oily stains—as the other two hung back.

"Problem here, boys?" came a new voice.

A bald man stood with his arms folded, muscles bulging—he looked like a cage fighter. Clipped to his belt was the gold shield of a detective with the Salt Lake PD.

"He saved your ass," the football player said, shoulder-checking Brigham as he walked away.

The detective paced the alley, waiting until the three men were out of earshot. "What the hell did you do to them, Brigham?"

"Nothing."

"He threw a plate of bruschetta," June offered.

The detective shook his head. "In my restaurant?"

"It was just tomatoes, Will."

"It's assault, dipshit. You're trying to become a lawyer—you can't have an assault charge on your record. And I own this fucking place and have to go explain to my customers that it wasn't a big deal. People want calm when they're eating, not fights."

"Sorry."

Will shook his head again and headed to the kitchen door in the back of the restaurant. Brigham chuckled, and June pushed him in the chest with both hands, making him stumble back.

"What?" he said.

"They were going to kick your ass."

"But they didn't."

"But they were going to."

"But they didn't. It's fine."

She sighed as though having to explain something to a child for the fiftieth time. "It's not fine, Brigham. You brought yourself down to their level. If you do that, you're no better than they are. All you had to do was ignore it, and they would've lost interest. Why did you have to do that?"

He shrugged. "I don't know. I'm sorry."

"Yeah, right."

"No, seriously—that was inconsiderate of me. I'm sorry. It won't happen again."

Her brow furrowed, and she appeared furious. Then, as quickly as it had come, the anger faded. She sighed again and took his arm. "Come on, dipshit. Let's go watch a movie."

Five

Brigham woke up early the next morning. He googled "law firms in salt lake city" and read down the list. At least thirty were within walking distance, and half a dozen were in the US Bank building that wasn't more than a mile from his house.

He only had one suit, which he'd bought secondhand from a place called Deseret Industries, and two ties. He wore his best white button-down shirt, which meant the only one without any stains, and shined his shoes with a damp paper towel. Brigham stared at himself in the mirror. He didn't look one bit like a lawyer. He looked like someone imitating a lawyer, who was worried everyone would see through him. It didn't matter, though—he had nothing else to do today.

The bike ride was short and easy, predominantly downhill, so he didn't even have to pedal and risk working up a sweat. The US Bank building was on Main Street, past the largest shopping mall in Utah, and across the street from Lamb's Grill—a place Brigham had always wanted to eat at but couldn't afford.

He locked his bike to a newspaper bin, got out six résumés, and went in. The first floor was all glass and shine. An old security guard was asleep at a black desk. Brigham sneaked past him to the list of tenants and memorized the floors with the law firms. Then he hopped on the elevators and went to the highest one, on the sixteenth floor.

The law firm had no walls, only glass. The carpets were white and clean and the windows went from floor to ceiling and looked down onto Salt Lake City. Noles, Valdo & Whittaker. Brigham strolled in confidently. It was fake confidence. He actually felt like he could vomit at any second. But he stood in front of the reception-ist, who looked up at him without smiling.

"Can I help you?"

"I'd like to speak to one of the partners, please."

"Which one?"

"I don't know. Whoever is in charge of hiring."

She looked him up and down as though he were a beggar asking for change. In some ways, he felt that way, too.

She called someone on her phone and said, "There's some guy here to talk to whichever attorney is in charge of hiring . . . Yeah . . . Yeah, okay." She hung up. "Just a moment."

The lobby was plush, and the paintings on the walls all looked as though they cost more than the house Brigham lived in. He could see through the glass back into all the offices and saw men and women in suits hurrying around, their coats off and their sleeves rolled up. Two older men were in a conference room with boxes of documents, a large plasma-screen television at the front of the room showing a PowerPoint slide.

"He'll see you now," the receptionist said.

Brigham followed the receptionist to an office in the back where a portly man sat behind a large desk. Documents were scattered everywhere—stacked on chairs, piled high on the desk, and stuffed onto shelves. The man was rubbing the bridge of his nose between red-rimmed eyes with dark circles below.

"What do you need?" he asked.

Brigham stepped forward. "My name's Brigham Theodore, sir. I've recently been sworn in to the Bar, and I'm looking for employment." He slid his résumé across the desk. "I've aced trial advocacy, as you can see. My grades aren't the best, but that's because I wanted to have a life, too." Brigham smiled, but when the man didn't, he stopped and cleared his throat. "Anyway—"

"Let me stop you right there, son. Trial ad's great, but no associates here go to trial. The partners handle that. Ten or fifteen years down the line, maybe we'd trust you with a trial. What we need associates for are research and writing—that's it. And the best researchers and writers are those in the top of their class, and only from certain schools. We recruit mostly from Harvard and Stanford. I'm afraid you'd have to be quite exceptional to compete with them."

"I understand that, sir, but I'd be willing to work for nothing until—"

"Sorry, we don't need anyone right now."

Brigham nodded and put out his hand to shake, but the man had gone back to his paperwork.

The next three law firms Brigham visited were nearly identical: mahogany paneling, attractive legal secretaries and paralegals, and attorneys who wouldn't give him the time of day. He didn't go to the right prep schools or belong to the right clubs. He wasn't one of "them." He was an outsider, and even offering to work for nothing wasn't enough to convince them to hire him.

So he decided to expand. He went to every law firm he could find—solo practitioners in basement offices, personal injury firms with offices just off the freeway and surrounded by billboards, social security disability firms that used clerks to do the work that attorneys should have been doing. No one was hiring. The only firm that showed interest, after he'd said he'd work for free, was a personal injury and medical malpractice firm operating out of a house that had been turned into offices. The man interviewing him, Matt something, was nice enough, and the offer of working for nothing perked him up.

But in the end, even they turned him down when one of the other partners informed Matt that they already had three law students working for nothing, and didn't need any more.

By afternoon, Brigham had been to over thirty law firms and had heard the same thing over and over: business was down, no one was hiring. The ones that were hiring only recruited from the top ten schools, and only wanted a certain type of associate. It was a club you had to be born into and couldn't join.

Brigham ate a donut in front of the public library downtown. The building was far more futuristic than the surrounding shelters and government-subsidized housing would lead someone to expect. It'd been built when the Olympics had come to Salt Lake in 2002 and was primarily used by the homeless now as a place to waste away the hours of the day. Five stories of glass sloped at an angle to give the impression of falling. Brigham had spent a lot of time there when studying for the bar, and the place felt comfortable to him.

As he finished the last of his donut, he glanced around and noticed a small set of offices. He'd seen them before and never taken notice. Now, they seemed like a glimmer of hope.

There was a sign in front of the building naming the tenants, and they included THE LAW OFFICES OF TTB. He threw the donut wrapper in a trash bin and headed across the street.

Above the entrance to the law firm was a neon sign that read ATTORNEYS AT LAW. Brigham stared at it a bit. It was an odd placement since the sign wasn't really visible from the street. Someone had just wanted neon above the door.

He went inside and tapped the bell on the counter at the receptionist's desk. After half a minute, an elderly woman stepped out from around the corner. She looked him up and down.

"Yes?"

"May I speak to the attorney in charge of hiring, please? Um, Mr. TTB if he's available."

"What do you want?"

"Well, ma'am, I'm a newly minted attorney and I'm here to offer my services."

She grimaced. "Hold on."

The woman stepped back around the corner, returning a moment later to tell him, "Go on back. First office to the left. Tommy is ready to see you."

Tommy, Brigham thought. Not Thomas. He liked this place already. He walked down a corridor and found the office, where a giant of a man sat at the desk. He was easily three hundred pounds, but not fat—not really; he looked more like a linebacker. His black cowboy boots were up on the desk and he wore a gold ring on every finger and both his thumbs. He had a ponytail despite the fact that the top of his head was balding. He had a phone against his ear. He held up one finger telling Brigham to wait, and then pointed to a chair in front of his desk.

"Yeah," Tommy said into the phone, "I get that. But he's lookin' at ten on the child porn charges anyway. So I don't think the gun charges matter. We're just gonna plead him. Yeah . . . yeah, okay . . . yeah, bye." Tommy hung up and glared at Brigham a moment before thrusting out his meaty hand. "Tommy Lenin, pleased to meet you."

Tommy had a thick Russian accent but every word was pronounced correctly. Brigham guessed he had studied English intensively for some time.

"Brigham Theodore."

"Brigham. I like the name, brother. So Kathy told me you're a new attorney."

"Yes, sir. Been licensed one day."

He smiled and took a cigar out of the desk followed by a gold lighter, which he used on the end. "That's great. Good decision, Brigham. Being a lawyer's a lotta fun. You get to fuck the government every now and again. You like fucking the government?"

"Um, well, I've never actually done it. But I'd like to."

"Excellent. Come outside with me."

Brigham rose and followed him. The people he saw on the way through the office were an odd assortment. Several men in short sleeves with wrinkled ties, a couple of young staff, and one woman he noticed, blonde and dressed far too elegantly for her surroundings, sitting in the largest office other than Tommy's. She glanced at him and then away again.

"Come on outside," Tommy repeated.

Once outside, Tommy sucked on his cigar and let the smoke whirl around him.

"See that there?" Tommy said, pointing to the building next door. "What do you see?"

"Um, a bail bonds agency."

"It's a gold mine is what it is, Brigham. That's how I make my bread. You see, all them uptight sonsabitches at the Bar don't know nothin' about what it's like to actually practice law. That's why they got all them ethical rules. Lawyers weren't even allowed to advertise until twenty years ago—we had to take it all the way to the fucking Supreme Court. So now they bind our hands to try and limit us."

"How so, sir?"

"Take personal solicitation. According to the Bar's ethical rules, a lawyer can't personally solicit business. Can't walk up to some poor bastard that's been in an accident and give him a card. I been reprimanded by the Bar sixteen times for that shit and nothing has stuck—not a one. But it takes time to fight 'em and earn a living. But now I got this," he said, looking over to the bail bonds agency. "I have them do all the soliciting and they only send clients to one law firm. You see what I'm saying? If you're gonna make it in this business, it's all about gettin' creative. You wanna fuck the government, but you also wanna hide from the Bar. Don't appear on their radar. You understand?"

"Yes, sir."

"Good." He stood staring at Brigham, drawing in a large mouthful of smoke, then blowing it out. "Go talk to Scotty. He'll get you set up. I get fifty percent of any case you bring in. Any case I give you, you get twenty-five percent. Fair?"

"Yes," he said. It certainly wasn't anything near fair, but he wasn't about to argue with the first job he'd gotten as an attorney.

Tommy headed back into the building. He stopped and looked at Brigham. "Welcome to the fire, kid."

Six

Brigham stood awkwardly in the middle of the office, people passing him without saying hello. He looked for the blonde woman he'd seen earlier, but he couldn't find her. There were probably a dozen lawyers; no one noticed that he was new.

Finally, a man as round as a basketball and wearing thick glasses stepped out of an office. He shuffled over and put out his hand, which still had chocolate stains on it—or at least what Brigham hoped were chocolate stains.

"You're Brigham, right?"

"Yeah."

"Nice to meet you. I'm Scotty. Everyone calls me that 'cause my name's Scott and I'm from Scotland. 'Cause o' *Star Trek*."

"Yeah, I figured."

"Lemme show you around."

They began the tour at reception. Scotty had a nervous tic and every once in a while his shoulder would twitch as he pointed people out and shouted their names. When they were out of earshot again, he'd tell Brigham something awful about them.

She had an abortion last year.

He likes to cheat on his wife with transsexuals.

He shoplifts for fun.

She got drunk once and blew a guy who turned out to be her uncle.

Brigham's initial impression of chaos and a disjointed staff vanished. He could see the theme now: All of these people were there because they didn't have better offers. Only the staff were salaried. Scotty told him the lawyers all had the same deal Brigham had been given.

Near the end, they'd reached the corner office where the blonde woman was drafting a document. Brigham's heart raced. He tried to appear as cool as he could by leaning against the wall, but his shoulder slipped, and he nearly fell over. The woman grinned.

"Hi, Brigham Theodore."

"Molly," she said.

"He's the new guy," Scotty chimed in.

"Well, welcome to the firm."

Scotty walked away but Brigham stood there, racking his brain for something, anything, to say. He noticed a collection of basketball trophies, and photographs on the wall.

"You played?" Brigham said.

"In college. You?"

"No, running was my sport."

She glanced back to her old photos. "If women had an even shot with men, I would have been able to go pro. But I abandoned it for law school because I thought that's what would lead me to the glamorous life."

"Has it?"

She chuckled. "I'm here, aren't I? But I can't complain. My class had a hundred and ten graduates and less than half of them have full-time employment. Take out the ones that aren't doing anything related to law and you've got a quarter of a law school class that are actually lawyers."

"Same with mine." He glanced down the hall at Scotty, who hadn't noticed Brigham wasn't there and was talking to himself.

"Tommy seems . . . interesting," Brigham said. "Why is it the 'Law Offices of TTB'?"

"He didn't tell you?"

Brigham shook his head.

"TTB stands for Tommy Two-Balls."

Brigham chuckled but stopped when he saw she was serious. "Why would he ever call his law firm that?"

"You'll have to ask him. A lot of rumors, but I doubt any of them are true."

Scotty yelled out, "Brigham, you comin'?"

"I'd better go," Brigham said to Molly. "Nice to meet you."

"You, too."

Brigham followed Scotty past the break room and to what looked like a utility closet.

"Your office," Scotty said. "Hang out for a minute and we'll get some work to you. Just drafting documents and stuff."

"Can I ask you something—do people here make good money?"

Scotty shifted from one foot to the other and Brigham got the impression he was uncomfortable. "Depends on them. If you hustle and get clients you'll do fine."

And with that, Brigham was left alone. The office had a desk and chair, but the desk appeared to be from an elementary school. He sat behind it and looked out the only window in the room to the parking lot. His view was of the last car in the row and a Dumpster.

He sighed, wondering why he'd chosen to go to law school in the first place. His degree was in biology. His college counselor had kept trying to talk him out of law school, saying that someone with a scientific mind wouldn't enjoy the work—unless he were to go into patent law, which Brigham had no interest in.

He stood up again and peeked outside the office. People were shouting into phones and others were speaking in hushed tones, recounting cases either won or lost. He went outside and turned around. He stared at the neon sign, then glanced over to the bail bonds place. A man who looked like the Terminator stepped out, got onto a Harley, and sped away.

Brigham strolled into the bail bonds office. A woman with a small dog sat behind the counter.

"Hi," he said. "I'm Brigham. I just got hired next door."

"Oh, another lawyer. You a young kid."

"Yes ma'am. Twenty-six."

"Why you wanna work for Tommy Two-Balls?"

"It's a job."

"You wanna know why he calls himself that, don't ya?" She shook her head. "The only person who knows is Scotty and he don't tell no one." She took out a stack of business cards and slid them to him. "You get a client that needs bail, you send 'em to me. For every client that you send me, I send one that needs a lawyer to you."

"Isn't that . . . I mean, don't the Bar ethics rules prohibit a mutual-referral plan with a non-lawyer?"

She stared at him for a moment in silence, and then burst out laughing.

"Thanks for the cards."

As he left, she was still laughing.

Seven

Brigham called Rick to let him know he'd found a job and would have to quit. Rick, rather than being upset, told him he was proud of him. They chatted a few minutes, and then said good-bye.

Brigham strolled around the office and talked with everyone. He figured they might have some extra work here and there to throw his way.

There was Mark, a former cop who said he'd gotten sick of lawyers yelling at him on the stand, so he'd quit and gone to law school. And Ryan, who struck Brigham as a psychopath—he was glib and trying much too hard to seem friendly and normal. He had been a trucker, but had become a lawyer because he didn't know what else to do. He specialized in small claims court and said he enjoyed it because most of the judges didn't know the laws and he could get away with anything. Sandy was a civil rights lawyer who sued businesses on behalf of minorities, and then kept a percentage of any recovery. Harold couldn't look Brigham in the eyes and kept his head down over his desk for the entire conversation, although Brigham did learn that he was a bankruptcy attorney.

And there was Molly. He couldn't figure out why she was there. She was beautiful, appeared smart but not so smart that she was weird, and probably could've used those two traits to land a job at a real law firm.

Brigham did one more round through the office, but no one mentioned any work so he went and sat at his desk and waited.

Scotty shuffled into Brigham's office toward the end of the day. He put a manila folder on Brigham's desk.

"Your first case. Tommy said to give it to you. Thousand-dollar fee so you'd get two fifty."

"What is it?"

"Speeding ticket." Scotty turned to leave. "Trial's tomorrow."

"Wait, I can't prepare for a trial in one night!"

Scotty stood awkwardly at the door and stared at his feet. "You did an internship, right? Where you tried cases?"

"Yeah, but I was supervised."

"It's just speeding—an infraction. The prosecutors knock stuff down to infractions 'cause you don't get a jury trial if it's an infraction. There's no jail time possible, so they do that with every case they can to save time. Bench trials only take a few minutes. You'll do fine."

Scotty left, and Brigham stared down at the manila folder. He opened it. Inside was an information sheet on the client. A one-page citation was attached naming the client as Jake Dolls, and saying he had been doing sixty-seven in a thirty. His wife had been the only passenger. The third page was a signed representation agreement . . . and that was it. There were no other notes. Brigham closed the file and turned to the desktop computer. It was at least fifteen years too old. He flipped it on and it took almost ten minutes of deep grinding noises to boot up. He went to the Internet Explorer icon and double-clicked. That took another few minutes to open. He turned the computer off and pulled out his iPhone. He googled "how to handle speeding tickets," found a few sites, and began reading.

The next morning, Brigham dressed in his suit again, and brought Jake Dolls's folder with him to the Salt Lake City Justice Court.

A line of people were waiting to go through a metal detector to get in, and belts, rings, and watches had to be removed. When people set the machine off, a bailiff pulled them aside and checked them with a wand. When it was his turn, Brigham's shoes set off the machine, and the bailiff took him aside and wanded him for a solid minute.

"I'm a lawyer," he said. "Can't I just go in?"

"No, we check you guys extra carefully."

Once he was cleared, he could see the sheer mass of humanity from every walk of life hurrying into the building. The courtroom he needed to be in, upstairs, was another zoo. At least ten defense lawyers were discussing their cases, with the prosecutors up front, and the audience benches were full. Brigham looked at the name on the file again and said loudly, "Jake Dolls?"

A man raised his hand and stood up. Brigham took him outside the courtroom.

"Jake, I'm Brigham Theodore. I'll be representing you today."

"Where's Tommy? I thought he was gonna be here."

"He sent me. I don't have any notes, so is there anything I should know?"

The man eyed him with his arms folded. "I told Tommy everything. He should be here."

Brigham put on his best smile. "Well, why don't you tell me? Let's start with your wife—she was in the car with you?"

"Yeah. She seen it, too. She was pregnant. Don't know if that matters but she was. We was just drivin', and then this cop come up behind me goin' really fast. So I go faster 'cause I think he's gonna hit me. Then he flashed his lights and pulled us over."

"Did you tell him you sped up because of him?"

"Yeah, and he didn't believe me. Made me wait the whole time with my wife screamin' at me while he gave me the ticket. That's really why I'm fightin' it—it ain't the money; I just don't think government should be able to do things like that and just get away with it."

Brigham nodded, making some quick notes on the back of the file with a pen that was running out of ink. "Okay. Let's go in."

Brigham moved past the bar—the actual physical barrier separating the crowd from the lawyers—to stand in the well before the judge's bench. If the judge had been on the bench, the bailiffs would have been required to tackle Brigham just for being there. As it was, he waited there with the other defense attorneys for his turn to talk to the prosecutor.

The prosecutor, a woman with black hair that came to her shoulders, was sitting at a table. Brigham smiled at her and said, "Hi, Brigham Theodore."

"What do you need?" she said curtly, not removing her eyes from the file in front of her.

"Um, I'm here for Jake Dolls. It's a—"

"There's no offer. He can plead guilty and pay the fine."

"Well, his wife was pregnant and—"

"He can plead guilty or we can have the trial."

"Okay, but—"

"Next."

Brigham felt someone gently pushing him out of the way, and another lawyer took his spot and tried convincing the prosecutor to give him a deal on a prostitution case. Brigham looked at Jake and could feel himself blushing. He went back to the defense table and sat on the bench behind it. Another lawyer sat there, a man in a suit with sneakers on. He was looking at his iPod, the earbuds dangling against his chest.

"She's a real ballbreaker," the man said.

"Seems like it."

"She won't give you anything. You gotta set everything for trial in here. But you get a free appeal."

"What'dya mean?"

"This is justice court—you get to appeal anything that happens to the district court. Starts the whole case over, so you get two bites at the apple. But when you appeal it, the judge can lock your client up. Still, Judge Bolson ain't so bad."

The bailiff said, "All rise. The Honorable Judge Zandra Bolson now presiding."

The judge was a middle-aged woman with curly hair. She sat, moved her files in front of her, and said, "You may be seated. Who's first?"

Every lawyer scrambled for the podium, fighting for a spot up there. The man with the iPod elbowed another lawyer in the chest, laughing, but Brigham could tell he meant it.

Brigham sat there for two and a half hours while the other lawyers handled their cases. Finally, his turn came at the podium. His heart felt as if it might rip out of his chest, and he was worried everyone was staring at how badly he was sweating. He gripped the podium hard to stop his hands from trembling.

"Matter of Jake Dolls, please, Your Honor."

Jake joined him at the podium. Brigham thought Jake must be the only person there more nervous than he was.

The judge opened a file. "Are you Jacob Ray Dolls, sir?"

"Yes."

"And is the address we have on the citation correct?"

"Yes."

"Okay, Counsel, what's anticipated?"

Brigham was staring at the charge sheet when the prosecutor cleared her throat. He glanced to her and she pointed to the judge.

"Oh, sorry, Your Honor. Um, what was that?"

"I said, what's anticipated?"

"We'll be going forward with the trial."

"Well, by all means, proceed," she said mockingly.

Brigham sat at the defense table, as did Jake. He wasn't sure which one it was until the bailiff pointed to it: the one farthest away from the jury box. He waited for the prosecutor to offer her opening statement, but she was busy on her phone. He thought maybe it was customary to let the defense go first at a bench trial.

Brigham had spent at least three hours preparing his opening statement. It couldn't be too long—judges probably hated that—but it couldn't be so short that it didn't seem like he cared about the case. So he'd written it, and then cut and trimmed until it was down to about five minutes.

"Your Honor, when our Constitution was written, the Founding Fathers sought to protect—"

"Mr. Theodore," the judge interrupted, "what're you doing?"

"Um, opening statement."

"We usually waive opening statements. It's a speeding ticket. I know what speeding is and what to expect."

"Oh. Right. Sorry, Your Honor."

"Your Honor," the prosecutor said, "the City calls Officer Walbot to the stand."

An officer in full uniform took the stand. He held up his right hand, and the clerk made him put his other hand on a Bible.

"Do you swear to tell the truth, the whole truth, and nothing but the truth, so help you God?"

"I do."

Once the officer was sworn in, the prosecutor went up to the podium and said, "State your name, please."

"Thomas J. Walbot."

"What do you do, Mr. Walbot?"

"I'm an officer with the Salt Lake City Police Department."

"How long have you been with them?"

"Ten years."

"And Officer, what were you doing on August fourth around ten in the morning?"

"I was patrolling the area of Fourth South and about State Street here in Salt Lake City."

The prosecutor had her phone out and was texting as she was asking questions. Brigham guessed she had done this several hundred times to get that comfortable. "And did you cite someone at that time?"

"Yes."

"Who?"

"The defendant. Jacob Dolls."

"Tell us what happened."

The officer leaned back in his seat, keeping his eyes on the prosecutor rather than the defendant. "I noticed a silver Honda coming down Fourth South at a high speed. I clocked him on my front ladar at sixty-seven miles—"

"Objection, Your Honor," Brigham said, his voice cracking a little. "The officer hasn't laid proper foundation."

The judge rolled her eyes. "Ms. Rollins, please lay the proper foundation."

The prosecutor glared at Brigham and then turned to the officer. "Do you have ladar in your vehicle, Officer?"

"Yes."

"What is ladar?"

"The word is a combination of *laser* and *radar*. You aim it at a spot and it lights it up, so it can then can read the reflecting light. It's completely replaced radar as a means of determining speed, because it's nearly a hundred percent accurate."

"Was your ladar working properly?"

"Yes."

"When was the last time you calibrated it?"

"That morning."

"And it was working properly?"

"Yes."

The prosecutor looked to Brigham as she said, "And you clocked the silver Honda at what speed with the ladar?"

"Sixty-seven. The posted speed limit in the area is thirty miles an hour."

"Did you identify the driver?"

"Yes."

"Do you see him in the courtroom today?"

The officer looked to Jake. "Yes. He's the man there, in the shirt and tie, next to defense counsel."

"How did you identify him?"

"His driver's license."

"Thank you, Officer. Nothing further."

Brigham swallowed, and his mouth felt like sandpaper. The judge didn't say anything, so he rose slowly and stepped over to the podium, waiting for someone to tell him it wasn't his turn yet.

"Officer," he said meekly, "you clocked him on your front ladar as you were following him, correct?"

"I saw that he was traveling at a high speed, so I followed him. I visually estimated his speed at sixty-five miles per hour."

"Visually estimated? That must have been some guess since you were only two miles per hour off."

"I received training on visual estimates at the academy. We're required to be accurate to within two miles per hour on our tests in order to pass."

Brigham hadn't known that and felt like everyone could see through him. He scribbled some nonsensical notes on his legal pad. "Um, how far away were you from his car?"

"Close."

"How close? Twenty feet?"

"Somewhere around there."

Brigham wanted to put a foot up on the lectern to seem more relaxed than he actually was, but he was shaking too much to manage it. No one would have seen it, anyway. "Were your lights on?"

"Yes."

"Your siren?"

"Yes, I believe so."

"And Mr. Dolls moved over to the side at first, right?"

"Yes. He pulled from the number one lane into the number two."

"But he didn't pull over and stop."

"Not right away."

Brigham glanced at the judge, who was on the computer. The screen was turned away so no one could see, but from her expression, it appeared she was watching something humorous—YouTube, maybe.

"So you have flashing lights and a siren, and he speeds up, and then pulls into the number two lane."

"I don't know if he sped up, but yeah, he pulled into the other lane."

"It's reasonable to say that if a speeding cop car is coming in behind you, you might speed up too, right?"

"I . . . I guess that's reasonable."

"Thank you. Nothing further."

The judge snapped out of whatever trance the computer had put her in and looked up at them. "Great. Closing arguments."

The prosecutor rose and was about to speak when Brigham said, "I'd like to call Mr. Dolls to the stand."

The prosecutor sighed audibly and sat back down. Jake rose and walked to the stand, sat down, and was sworn in as the officer had been. Brigham stayed at the lectern. Jake looked so nervous that Brigham mouthed the words *It's fine* at him.

"Please state your name," Brigham said.

"Jacob Dolls."

"And Mr. Dolls, you heard the officer's testimony relating to the events on August fourth?"

"Yes."

"Is his account accurate?"

"Not really. What happened was I was coming down the hill, there's this hill right there before Pioneer Park, and he comes up behind me. Like, *right* behind me. He said around twenty feet but I'd say more like ten. And his siren wasn't blarin' yet, so I thought he was tryin' to pass me. So I sped up, 'cause if I woulda hit my brakes, he woulda rammed into me. Then when them sirens turned on, I changed lanes to give him a clear road."

Brigham nodded. "Would you have been speeding otherwise?"

"No."

"Thank you, nothing further." Brigham sat back down.

The prosecutor was on her phone again. She rose, looked at Jake, and asked one question. "Were you speeding in Salt Lake on August fourth?"

"Well, yeah, but I said why."

"Thank you. Nothing further."

Jake walked through the well back to his seat. Speeding was a strict liability offense, meaning there was no element of intent. It didn't matter if your house was on fire or your pregnant wife was delivering in the backseat. If you were speeding, you were guilty. And Jake had just admitted that he had been speeding.

"Your Honor, I'd like to call Sandra Dolls to the stand," Brigham said.

Jake's wife was wearing a strapless dress. Her figure was slim and muscular, and Brigham wished he'd known she would be wearing that. He would have told her to wear a sweatshirt and glasses instead. Something that didn't scream *partier* to the judge.

He went through the same questions with Sandra as he had with Jake and she testified identically. They had not been speeding until the officer got behind them. The prosecutor had no questions for her, and Brigham rested.

"Closing arguments," the judge said.

The prosecutor said, "Waive closing."

Brigham rose again. "Your Honor, Mr. Dolls was entrapped. He was traveling at a normal speed until this officer got behind him.

Mr. Dolls and his wife both testified that they were traveling at a normal speed, the officer got behind them, and they sped up to avoid a collision. For entrapment, we have to show that the defendant was enticed or encouraged into doing something the defendant would not have otherwise done. Mr. Dolls would not have sped except for the officer's actions."

The prosecutor rose, anger flashing across her face. "Your Honor, entrapment requires providing the City with notice of an affirmative defense ten days prior to trial."

"There's an exception for infractions," Brigham said, thumbing through the court's copy of the *Utah Code Annotated* that sat on the defense table. He found the entrapment statute. "Um, may I approach?"

"Yes," the judge said.

Brigham crossed the well with the prosecutor right behind him. He set the thick book before the judge and pointed to a section at the bottom of the page. "It states that notice is only required when incarceration is possible. No incarceration is possible on an infraction."

The judge read it and looked at the prosecutor. "Ms. Rollins, any response?"

"Entrapment is when an officer puts someone in a situation where they are coerced into committing a crime. The defendant didn't have to speed. He could've kept his pace."

"And the officer might've rear-ended him."

"That's bullshit."

The judge held up a hand. "All right, everybody calm down. It's a traffic ticket. Get on back and I'll make my ruling."

Brigham glanced to the bailiff as he sat down. A few lawyers were still in the courtroom behind him, and one gave him a thumbs-up. The officer glared at Brigham. Jake leaned over and whispered, "Did we win?"

"I don't know."

"I'm prepared to make my ruling," the judge said, writing something down on the court's file. "It was a nice shot, Mr. Theodore, but I don't see entrapment here. The officer has to have the intent to encourage the defendant to commit the crime. I didn't hear any evidence that indicated to me that he had that intent. When defense counsel makes a motion for entrapment, the burden then shifts to them to prove by a preponderance of the evidence that entrapment did in fact occur. We don't have that here. So I do find the defendant guilty of the offense of speeding. But I'll give you this—it was original. I've never heard that defense applied to speeding before." She turned to Jake. "Mr. Dolls, you have up to forty days to come back and receive sentence, or you may waive the forty days and be sentenced today. Which do you prefer?"

"Today, please."

"All right. I am imposing a fine of two hundred sixty-three dollars, and an order of six months' good behavior probation—that means no new traffic tickets. You get a new one within six months, and you'll have to come back here and explain to me why, Mr. Dolls."

"Yes, ma'am."

Brigham was staring straight ahead. He couldn't look at Jake. Instead, he gathered his things and hurried out. Jake followed him and Brigham realized he wasn't going to be able to sneak away, so he turned to face him.

"Thanks," Jake said, brushing past him. "Asshole," Jake muttered when he was a few steps away.

Eight

Night fell quickly, and Brigham sat at home on his couch and stared at the television screen. He hadn't gone back to the office after his loss that morning. He couldn't face Tommy. The man had trusted him, and Brigham had failed him on his first try. Tomorrow, he would go back to the school and beg for his old job back.

As he put a beer to his lips, the doorbell rang. Brigham answered, and Scotty and Tommy stood there.

Tommy glanced past him inside. "We gotta get you a better pad, Brigham."

"Oh, um, you guys want to come in?"

"No," Tommy said, wiping his nose with the back of his index finger. "Let's go out."

Brigham grabbed his jacket and wordlessly followed the two men out of his building. They were discussing a personal injury case, something about a woman who had been hit in a crosswalk. Scotty wanted to settle for a hundred thousand, but Tommy thought they could get double that if they held out.

A black Mercedes was parked out front, and Tommy drove. Brigham sat in the back and tried to think of what to tell him about why he'd lost. All he could think to do was apologize and let Tommy know he'd be quitting.

"I'm sorry about today," Brigham said.

"Sorry?" Tommy asked without looking back. "About what?"

"Losing."

Tommy laughed and Scotty snorted.

"Brigham, I talked to one of the lawyers who was there. He said you argued entrapment. I've never heard an entrapment defense on a speeding ticket. That's creative thinking right there."

"Yeah, but I lost."

"What do you think the national average is for not-guilty verdicts?"

"I don't know. Fifty percent."

"It's twenty-five percent. That means we lose three in every four trials. The prosecutor's got all the evidence before we do, so they only bring the cases they think they can win, which keeps their success rate up. Then you got cops willing to lie on the stand, and the ones that aren't willing to lie are willing to embellish the truth. On the other side, you got our clients, most of whom have criminal records and no juries or judges believe anything they say. The system is stacked against us from the get-go. You gotta get used to losing, or else you ain't gonna make it. Besides, Jake's probably going to appeal the loss. Another thousand bucks for us."

Brigham had had a knot in his stomach since that morning, but it slowly faded away. He relaxed into the leather seats and stared out the windows.

"So I'm not fired?"

The two men laughed again. "Fired? Hell, I'm promoting you."

Brigham looked to him. "Promoting me to what?"

"We'll talk tomorrow. Tonight, let's just have fun."

They went to a downtown bar that had a pig painted on the wall. Tommy parked the Mercedes on the street and they walked in. The bouncer nodded at Tommy, and Tommy nodded back. Once they were inside, he said, "Former client. Got him a great deal on a drug charge."

They sauntered up to the bar and Tommy ordered three shots of whiskey. The bartender was a shapely woman with big, fake breasts, and Scotty was staring at them like they were the Pyramids of Giza.

Tommy held up his shot glass and Scotty did the same. Brigham had already drunk his but he held it up and tried to cover it with his hand so they couldn't see that it was empty.

"To hopefully."

They shot the booze and Tommy motioned for refills. A man sat in the corner with his arms folded, and the two of them exchanged glances.

"Be right back," Tommy said.

When he was gone, Scotty and Brigham shot the refills, with Scotty, who seemed to be relaxing, taking two. His awkward manner had softened and he even smiled at the bartender and commented on her hair.

"What does that mean?" Brigham said. "'To hopefully?'"

Scotty ordered two beers. "Don't totally know. Tommy's been saying it forever."

"Who's that guy he went back there with?" Brigham asked.

"Client. This place is owned by the Russian mob, and some of them are our clients."

"Really?"

Scotty nodded, his shoulder twitching as he took a sip of his beer. "Bought and paid. Bars are good places to launder money 'cause no one keeps track of tips. On paper, half a dozen bigwigs in the Russian mob work here as bartenders and waiters. You give each bartender five or six hundred bucks a night in tips, each waiter a few hundred, and before you know it you got fifty or sixty grand a month in clean money. They claim it on their taxes so you gotta pay that, but so what? What else you gonna do with it? Works out nice."

Tommy was gone for a long while, and when he came back out he laid three hundred-dollar bills on the bar. "You boys have fun," he said. "I'll see you tomorrow, Brigham. And we'll talk about that promotion."

Brigham watched him leave. It seemed like everyone, from the cocktail waitresses to the managers, respected Tommy. He wondered what someone would have to do to get people already in the Russian mob to respect you.

"You liked Molly, didn't you?"

Brigham looked to Scotty, who had a mischievous grin on his face. "Was I that obvious?"

He shrugged. "She's a man-eater, though. I've never seen her with a guy. I think she scares people."

"She seemed nice enough."

"You haven't seen her pissed off yet. I saw her tear a cop apart on the stand once—it was so bad he started crying right there in the courtroom."

Brigham sipped his beer. A young woman smiled at him from across the bar. He smiled back, but knew he wasn't interested.

"What's the promotion he was talking about?" Brigham asked.

Scotty sipped his beer, his eyes twinkling as he smiled. "You're gonna love it."

Nine

Brigham rose early and went for a run through the Avenues. Though the Avenues themselves were congested, if he headed north up the mountain he came to a trail around to the other side with an open view of the valley below.

A solid forty minutes got him to the pinnacle of the first mountain, overlooking Davis and Weber counties, two counties dominated by industry. Several factories and oil refineries were spewing thick, gray exhaust into the sky. The acidic clouds whirled and danced in the wind, hovering above the cities and leaving a sour taste in the air before eventually dissipating.

Brigham jogged back home and changed. He would need to buy another suit as soon as he had some money. Checking his bank balance on his phone, he saw he had exactly nine hundred and fifty-two dollars left. His rent was three fifty, so as long as he ate corn dogs and Top Ramen, he had enough to live on for two months.

At work, he was passing Tommy's office when Tommy shouted, "Brigham, come here."

He went in and sat down across from him. Tommy removed a check from the printer and gave it to him. It was for two hundred fifty dollars.

"Twenty-five percent of the speeding case," Tommy said.

It was more money than he earned in a week cleaning the school, and it had only taken him a few hours to make. There was a warm sensation in his gut that he didn't recognize—maybe something between satisfaction and the beginnings of greed, for someone who had never felt greedy. He pushed it away with the thought that ten percent of it would have to go immediately to charity: a lesson his mother had taught him. If people gave as soon as they earned, it would keep them humble, as his mother had told him at least once a week. Brigham had stuck to it his entire life.

"Got something else, too," Tommy said. "Your promotion." From the floor behind his desk, he lifted up a box with several files and shoved it across to Brigham. There was also a padded envelope in there with at least twenty CDs.

"What is it?" Brigham asked.

"Your new case," Tommy said, lighting a cigar. "Amanda Pierce. I have a public defender contract with the county, and they send us things every now and then. Ten thousand for the case and fifteen hundred a day for the trial, plus you get all the experts and investigators that you need, all paid for by the state."

Brigham looked up at him, not sure what to say. Some quick math told him that was $2500 for the case and $375 a day for the trial: more money than he'd ever earned at one time.

"What's she charged with?"

"Murder, my friend. Aggravated murder, actually—part of the code says if you create a great risk of death to a person other than the victim and the actor, they bump murder up to aggravated murder. She's lookin' at the death penalty."

Brigham became aware of the dryness of his mouth; his tongue was stuck to his teeth, and he tried to swallow, but it felt like his throat had closed up. He finally managed to work his tongue loose and said, "I don't think I can do this, Tommy."

"Sure ya can."

"The only case I've ever handled by myself was that speeding ticket yesterday, and I lost."

Tommy shook his head. "It's all elements. Criminal Law 101: every crime has elements the prosecutor must prove, whether it's speeding or murder. You pick the element you got the best shot at beatin', and you attack it like a pit bull. Don't matter what the underlying charge is."

"Can I . . . think about it, at least?"

"Do this for me—go visit her. Right now. You can't be at the jail during mealtime, but you should be able to make it before then. Go visit her, and then tell me what you want to do."

Brigham nodded absently, staring at the thick file in front of him. "Go visit her?"

"Yup."

He rose, slipping out the first page in the file covering the charges and a summary of the allegation. "All right, I'll visit her."

Tommy took a puff of his cigar. "Come see me after."

Brigham left the office and googled the Salt Lake Metro Jail. It was a good distance away. At times like these, he wished he could afford a car. He got on his bike and turned onto State Street anyway.

The distance gave him time to think. This was ludicrous. He wasn't prepared for a murder case, and certainly not one in which the client was looking at the death penalty. He would have a quick meeting with this lady, hear her story, and then assure her that Tommy would take care of everything. Then he would ask Tommy for more speeding cases.

The jail was on the corner of an intersection. He could see nothing but dirt fields and empty parking lots farther down the road. As Brigham rode up, he saw there was no place to lock up his bike. He took it inside and leaned it against the wall.

A row of jail staff in uniform sat behind a counter. He went to the farthest one on the right, designated for professional visits. Taking out his Bar ID card, he watched the woman behind the counter. She wasn't paying the slightest bit of attention to him.

"Um, excuse me? I need to visit one of my firm's clients—Amanda Pierce."

"What cell block is she in?"

"I don't know."

The woman sneered. "Hold on."

She ran through a few queries on a computer before speaking into a microphone and asking someone to bring out Amanda Pierce for a professional visit. She examined his ID card, then handed it back and pointed to the metal detectors. "Through there. Cell block D One."

Brigham was shown one of the small lockers that were available to everyone visiting an inmate. He placed his keys, wallet, and phone inside, and then went through the metal detectors, got wanded a good half a minute, and then continued on. He turned toward the D cell block and continued down a concrete corridor.

The corridor was painted gray and yellow. The only decorations up in the hallways were the artwork that the inmates made themselves: drawings of nude women riding stallions, of Aztec kings, vanquishing conquistadors, of death and sex.

Brigham came to a cul-de-sac. The doors were lettered and numbered, and he pressed the buzzer for D-1. The door clicked open and he went in.

Metal stools stood before glass partitions. On the other side of the first one sat a woman. Her hair was down to her shoulders and she looked frail, as though she could collapse from exhaustion or malnutrition at any moment. The woman glanced at him and then looked down. He thought she had been crying recently.

Brigham sat down across from her. "Hello," he said.

"Hi," she said shyly, not looking up.

She looked nothing like what Brigham had pictured. He had been imagining tattoos and needle marks from meth. What he got was a frightened housewife in a world she couldn't possibly belong in. She had a cast on her left wrist and the fingers of that hand looked swollen and red.

"Um, my name is Brigham Theodore. I'm with the law offices of Tommy . . . well, TTB Law Offices. We've been assigned your case as part of the public defender contract."

She nodded. "Okay."

"I read the information and it alleged that you shot and killed a Tyler J. Moore."

She nodded. Brigham waited for her to say something else, but she just sat there quietly. When she finally did look up, her eyes held a palpable pain and sadness that got to him.

"Um, do you deny that, Ms. Pierce?"

"No," she said.

Brigham skimmed the file, which consisted of two sheets of paper. "The report said that you didn't confess, which is good, but I did read that, at the time, Mr. Moore had been facing charges of child abduction, forcible sodomy, and murder for the death of—"

Brigham stopped when he heard her make a sound. He looked up from the file. Her hand covered her face, and her slumped shoulders jolted with each sob. He read the rest of the report quietly. It stated that the victim in Tyler Moore's case was an underage relative of Amanda Pierce with the initials TP.

"I'm sorry," he said.

She shook her head and wiped the tears away. Brushing her hair aside, she raised her eyes to his. "She was my daughter. Tabitha."

Brigham nodded. The entire thing came into focus now. He had pictured a jilted lover or a bingeing meth addict killing someone who had wronged her . . . but he hadn't made the connection that Tyler

Moore had been killed because of the victim he had chosen. Brigham guessed the information only had initials because the victim was a juvenile. "How old was she?"

"Six. Almost seven."

Brigham glanced through the rest of the charges that Tyler Moore had faced. Aggravated sexual abuse of a child: five counts; forcible sodomy: two counts; rape of a child: three counts; aggravated kidnapping of a child: one count; aggravated mayhem: four counts; aggravated murder: one count.

As the last moments of Tabitha Pierce's life became clear, cold revulsion swept through him. He tried desperately to push the images away, to think of something else, but he couldn't. He looked at her mother. Her eyes were focused on his.

"I . . ." Brigham wanted to say something comforting, something that would reassure her. But no words came. Instead, he just said, "I'll be defending you. I'll come back tomorrow with my laptop to take notes, and we can go through what happened in detail. I just wanted to meet you."

She nodded, still wiping away the tears on her cheeks. "Thank you," she said softly. She rose, and Brigham saw the missing leg, the crutch leaned against the wall that Amanda placed under one arm as she pounded on the steel door with the other. The door slid open and a guard came and got her.

Brigham sat in the room, staring at the glass divider that had separated him from her. He read the list of charges in front of him, charges that represented a nightmare for a little girl, and felt the warmth of a tear down his cheek. He wiped it away and rose, leaving the jail and heading back to the office for the file.

Ten

Brigham sat in his office with his feet up on the desk, balancing the folder on his lap.

Amanda Pierce was only twenty-eight years old, and the state was looking to put her to death: she would be the first woman ever executed in Utah.

She had worked at a Walmart part time as a cashier, and her file said she had received disability payments from the government. She had been a private in the army medical supply line. She had been injured during her first three months stationed in Kandahar, Afghanistan, and she had lost her left leg below the knee. She wore a prosthetic, but seemed to be having trouble adjusting to it.

She had an ex-husband, Tabitha's father, who was currently living in California. He had been convicted of domestic violence and violation of a protective order. Brigham saw on a court docket that he had served ninety days in jail and then moved to Los Angeles. Tommy's investigator had tried to contact him, but he said, and the investigator made sure to quote this: "I don't give a shit 'bout either o' them whores." Amanda had no other living relatives.

The police reports in the case were only five pages in total. Brigham couldn't tell if that was normal or not, but thought that a homicide might require more, given that the speeding ticket had been one page. The case, according to the detective on scene, was open and shut. Five rounds into the victim, one round missing him and found embedded in a tree behind him while another round ricocheted off the curb. Amanda then dropped the weapon before the deputies transporting the prisoner tackled her. One of them dislocated Amanda's wrist, which explained the cast.

The detectives had taken her back to the station and interrogated her, but she didn't say anything. Didn't even ask for a lawyer. She just sat at the table and wept. The file included a DVD of the interrogation, and Brigham pulled it out. He pushed it into his laptop and watched as the detective strolled into the room and sat across from a trembling Amanda Pierce.

"Ms. Pierce, you need to talk to me. I can understand why you did what you did. I woulda put a bullet in him myself. But you need to tell me why, so I can help you with the DA. Do you understand? I'm here to help. Just tell me you did it and why, and we can talk about getting the DA down here to talk about deals. What do you say?"

Amanda stared at the floor. Even on the grainy video, Brigham could see her hands shake and the tears that flowed down her cheeks. At one point, she put her head down on the table and sobbed. The detective closed his binder and left the room.

Brigham looked at the autopsy photos. The only dead people he'd ever seen were in movies. And none of them had been through an autopsy. The man was rough looking and the one thing that struck him was how dirty Tyler Moore's socks were before the autopsy. For some reason, that disgusted him more than the autopsy.

The pathologist had cut him open, peeled his face off, removed his brain, and all manner of other horrible things that Brigham did not understand the reason for. He could only stomach a few photos before flipping through the rest of the file, which was mostly supplemental narratives of the follow-up investigation that the detectives had done, CAD call logs to dispatch, and criminal histories and court dockets for Tyler and Amanda.

Brigham went to the small library the Law Offices of TTB maintained in a room no bigger than his bedroom. He then took out the *Utah Rules of Criminal Procedure*, sat at a table, and began reading.

He read the rules and then the cases associated with the rules in the annotations. He read an entire transcript of a homicide trial similar to his that he found on Xchange, the Utah court case information system. He read motions filed by attorneys in that case and several others, and he read several blog entries written by defense attorneys relating to capital cases.

Then he dug into *Mangrum and Benson on Utah Evidence*, and read every relevant rule and the associated cases out of Utah.

By the time he was done, he looked out the window and it was pitch-black outside. The clock on his phone said it was nearly midnight. He stood up, stretched, and went home.

June didn't open her door when he went in. She was dating a couple of guys. Once, she had introduced Brigham to one of them and it was awkward for both of them. After that, she didn't introduce him anymore.

Brigham went down to his room and collapsed onto the bed without even bothering to slip out of his clothes. Then he remembered that he was supposed to inform Tommy whether or not he was taking the case. He felt his pockets for his cell phone and then just sent a single text: *I'll do it.*

The next couple of days were a blur of research and coffee-fueled all-nighters. He read a treatise by someone named Judge Boyce about how the rules of privilege related to capital cases and several other treatises on how capital cases were different in scope from homicide cases in which the death penalty wasn't on the table.

And then he came across a book by a law professor out of Berkley on mental health defenses in capital cases. The book was less than three hundred pages and Brigham read it twice in four days. The only breaks he took were to eat, use the bathroom, and speak briefly with Scotty, who was a nice guy, but even the most basic legal concepts confused him. Scotty quickly found that he could ask Brigham about any issues he had and save himself hours of research.

Tommy had been gone for the past three days. Scotty said he disappeared sometimes, probably on trips to visit some of the clients he had overseas. One night, Scotty brought a bottle of bourbon and two glasses into the library and poured one for Brigham. They sat and drank and talked about the firm.

"What kind of clients does Tommy go and check on overseas?" Brigham asked.

"The kind you shouldn't know about for plausible deniability."

"Ah."

"Yeah."

"Can I ask you something, Scotty? Why does he go by the nickname Tommy Two-Balls?"

Scotty's face turned serious and he leaned close. "I have to invoke attorney-client privilege on this. Assuming you're my attorney."

"I won't tell anyone."

Scotty glanced out the door and listened quietly a few moments. "He's Russian, you know. Tommy's not his real name. It's Taras. Taras Fokin. Supposedly, he was in the mob before he moved to America, but he left it when he went to law school—left the whole thing, and no one just decides to leave them. It's bad for their reputation. So one night, some guys broke into his house and cut off one of his balls. They didn't kill him 'cause he'd earned a lot of respect, but they couldn't let him off, either."

"So why two balls, then?"

"You didn't let me finish. So he, again, supposedly, found the guy that had done it. And Tommy ripped his ball off and had a surgeon put it inside him."

Brigham was quiet a moment. "That is the stupidest thing I've ever heard."

He shrugged. "It's what they say."

"Did Tommy tell you that?"

"No. He doesn't talk about it. Ever. So don't ask."

Once Scotty had left, Brigham went back to studying. It was amazing to him how little he had actually learned in law school. Even simple things, like what the different court hearings in a criminal case were called, or where to file different motions.

It was morning by the time he finished. He went home and managed to sleep for four hours before showering and heading back to the office.

Eleven

Brigham sat in his office and read through the Amanda Pierce file again. He read every word in the detective's reports until he knew them by heart. He watched the interview over and over until he felt he knew Amanda. And then he realized he hadn't visited her in jail like he said he would. He put a reminder in his calendar to visit her the next day.

He closed the file and looked out his window to the parking lot. A tree was swaying with the wind. A few clouds dotted the sky but didn't completely block out the sun. The temperature was warm and it almost lulled him to sleep.

"Murder? Seriously?"

He looked over and saw Molly Becker leaning against his door-frame. "I know."

"You're not ready for that."

"I know."

"Did you tell him you couldn't do it?"

He shook his head. "No, I said I would."

She was quiet a moment. "This isn't a game, Brigham. Someone's life is in your hands."

"I know."

"Then what makes you think you can go up against a prosecutor that has twenty years' experience on you? I know Vince Dale. He's an attack dog. Why do you think you're ready?"

He shrugged, looking back out the window. "I don't know."

She scoffed. "That's not an answer. I'm talking to Tommy about taking you off this."

She disappeared, leaving him alone. He flipped through the file again, and then decided he needed to go for a walk.

The temperature outside was warmer than it had been inside, so he took off his jacket and carried it, heading for a nearby coffee shop. He passed the library, the groups of homeless youths lounging on the green lawn, and construction sites on a new public-safety building.

The coffee shop was two floors and quiet, with photos of native coffee farmers from South America on the walls. It was the type of place that tried to make you feel guilty if you bought your coffee anywhere else, even though they probably didn't do anything different than Starbucks.

He got a vanilla steamer and climbed the steps to the second floor, taking a seat at a table by the window looking down onto Main Street. He watched a few transients loitering around Trax, the inner city train. Buses didn't run often down here anymore. Brigham took out his phone and dialed home.

"Brigham!" His mother was probably beaming; he could tell just by the sound of her voice. "I was just thinking about you."

"How are you, Ma?"

"I'm great. When you texted me and said you got sworn in, I told Claudia that you got sworn in to the Bar and you're a lawyer now. She said to tell you she's really proud of you."

"Tell her thanks."

"So how's everything going?"

"Fine. I guess. I got a job."

She gasped. "Already!"

"It's not a big deal, Ma. It's kind of an eat-what-you-kill place."

"But still, they must have seen somethin' in you to hire you so quick." She paused. "I'm sorry I couldn't be there. I just couldn't swing the money."

"You don't have to apologize. Do you need anything? I don't have much but I could send a few bucks."

"Don't be silly, son. We're fine." She exhaled loudly. "I'm so proud of you, Brigham."

"Thanks, Ma. I just wanted to check in. I'll call you later."

"Okay. Love you."

"Love you, too."

Molly came tramping up the stairs just as he was putting his phone down on the table. She sat across from him and folded her arms.

"How'd you find me?"

"I followed you. You're not ready for a murder case."

"I've already agreed with you."

"Then why are you doing it?"

He leaned forward on his elbow, staring into the foamy top of the steamer. "I don't know."

"You don't even know her."

He took a thin red straw from a dispenser on the table and swirled it in the drink. "When I was ten years old, my parents got into a huge fight. Don't even remember what it was about. They don't either. But my mom stormed outta the house, got on her bike, and took off. There was this park by our house and even though it was like ten at night, she went through there to clear her head . . . she remembers a white light, and a pain in the back of her head. When she woke up, she was naked and bleeding. She had, like, cigarette burns over her body. Two homeless guys had beaten and raped her."

He looked up and her eyes were glued to him.

"I'm sorry," she said.

"I know how Amanda Pierce felt. That hopelessness, the pain that no one else can feel. I was right there with her."

She sighed and rested her hands on the table. "You could let someone else handle it."

"What'll happen to the case if I turn it down?"

"Tommy will assign it to someone else."

"You?"

"No."

"Is there anyone in that office who would care about it as much as I do?"

She was silent a moment. "You're going to need help."

"I'll take whatever I can get."

Twelve

Tommy's investigator leased a space in downtown Salt Lake City next to an adult novelty shop. Brigham sat in the passenger seat of Molly's Chrysler 300, impressed by how clean she kept it.

"Can I ask you something?" he said.

"Why am I with Tommy?" she guessed.

"You seem like the big corporate lawyer type."

"And spend a hundred hours a week with bosses that just see me as a pair of tits? I'll pass. Tommy respects me. He sends me enough work where I'm busy but this isn't my life."

"What is your life then?"

She glanced to him. "Triathlons."

"Seriously?"

"Yes, seriously. I've done twelve. My thirteenth is in a month in Saint George. You ever competed?"

"No. I boxed for a little bit as a kid. Just some stuff my daddy taught me, and I competed in that. I run every day, though. How'd you get into triathlons?"

"I wanted something challenging that I had to work on every day. You can't fake your way through a triathlon. You have to put in the preparation or you'll die out there. The building's right here."

The building was red brick, right next to a neon palace. The adult store had dildos, mannequins dressed in lingerie, and boxes of pornography stacked behind thick glass. With the flashing lights, it looked like a circus.

"The investigator's here?"

"The best investigators are the ones willing to get their hands dirty. And Kris is certainly willing to get his hands dirty."

They walked into the office of A Plus Investigators. The interiors of the office walls were brick, just like the outside. Leather furniture was crowded into the waiting room, with several magazines on the coffee table. Molly went up to the reception desk and asked for Kris, and moments later a man strolled out from the back. He wore a suit that seemed to shine underneath the lights, and gold lit his black skin wherever possible—gold bracelets, rings, necklace, and even golden-toed cowboy boots.

"Molly, what's up, baby? How you doin'?"

"I'm good. This is Brigham, Tommy's newest."

"Brigham, my man, how you doin'?"

"Good, thanks." They shook hands and Brigham smelled the overpowering scent of expensive cologne applied liberally.

"Somethin' to drink? Coffee, soda? Somethin' harder?"

"We're good," Molly said. "We just wanted to talk to you about a case you did the prep work on. Amanda Pierce."

"Oh, right. Yeah. Well, come on back."

They followed him down a hallway. On the walls hung posters of outlaws from the twenties and thirties, like Al Capone and John Dillinger. His office had the same décor with the addition of Kris posing with several celebrities in photos hanging behind his desk.

"So what you wanna know?" he said, taking a seat in his leather chair.

Brigham sat down and put his hands on the armrests. They were greasy. He hoped whoever had sat there before just had a lot of lotion on. "I read your report. I was just wondering if there was anything else we need to look into."

"Anything else like what?"

"She shot someone in broad daylight. I think the only defense we're going to have is a type of temporary insanity."

He nodded. "That's something. Better than getting up in front of a jury with your dick in your hands, I guess."

"Only about one percent of insanity defenses work, Brigham," Molly said. "I think we need to try using sympathy to get the prosecution to give us second-degree manslaughter."

"She could still serve fifteen years for that."

"It's better than the death penalty."

Kris stared at Brigham a moment. Brigham presumed he was sizing him up for something, but couldn't guess what. "How old are you?"

"Twenty-six."

"And how many felonies you handled?"

"Um, none."

He shook his head. "Even the public defenders work a few years before gettin' a homicide, man."

"I can handle it."

He shrugged. "Up to you. Just make sure Molly or Tommy is backin' you every step. So what you wanna know about her mental health?"

"I'd like to find any friends, neighbors, churchgoers, anyone that knows her, who can testify to her mental state after her daughter was killed."

Kris made a note on a legal pad. "Anything else?"

"That's it for now. I'm going to go visit her again so I'll let you know if there's anything else."

"All right, man. I'll keep you posted. You got balls, I'll give you that."

"Thanks."

They rose and walked out. Once in the car, Molly put the keys in the ignition before she paused, turning and looking at him.

"What?" he said.

"I think we need to go for manslaughter."

"I'll talk to her about it."

"I'm serious, Brigham."

"So am I. I'll bring it up and if that's what she wants us to do, that's what we'll do."

Molly dropped him off at the jail and left to attend a mediation on a divorce case. Brigham stood outside the jail and watched as several groups of people walked out: families visiting loved ones, a few of them crying. One little boy held a picture drawn in crayon that said, "I love you dad."

He walked inside and the same clerk was working. The line was so long that it took her a good twenty minutes to get to him and call down to the cells to get Amanda Pierce ready for a visit.

Once through the metal detectors, Brigham walked more confidently down the hallway, ignoring the drawings on the wall. The first visit had been like landing on an alien planet. But the anxiety had diminished and he hoped with a few more visits he wouldn't feel so out of place.

Amanda was already sitting at a counter when he got there. Her hair was pulled back in a clip. When she saw him, a weak smile cracked her dry lips.

"How are you holding up?" Brigham asked. He had read on one attorney's blog he should never ask an inmate how they were doing because the answer was always "shitty."

"Okay. Thank you for seeing me again."

"It's no problem. I wanted to go through some things with you." She nodded. "First, I've reviewed everything in the case several times,

Amanda. A colleague of mine who is helping with this case has reviewed it, too. She thinks we should try and negotiate a deal to get the charges reduced to second-degree manslaughter."

"What does that mean?"

"Manslaughter is where you kill somebody but you didn't mean to."

"But I did mean to."

He paused, her bluntness taking him aback. "I know. But it's what's called a legal fiction. We're all just going to assume you didn't and you'll enter a guilty plea to the manslaughter."

"So how long would I be in jail?"

"You wouldn't be in jail. Jail is only for people awaiting trial or serving misdemeanor sentences less than a year. You'd be transferred to the Utah State Prison. For a second-degree felony, you'd serve one to fifteen years. Manslaughter can also be a first-degree felony and that'd be six to life. But we're shooting for a second. It'd be up to the parole board how much of that you actually served."

She nodded. "I understand."

"The other option is we can fight it. We can go to trial and do everything we can to win."

"But if we lose, I could die?"

He nodded. "Yes. The state has filed a notice saying they're looking for the death penalty."

She sighed, running her hand over her forehead and into her hair. "I don't care either way. I don't . . . I don't want to think about this anymore. So, I'll take the manslaughter."

"Are you sure? Once you enter a plea to something like that you won't be able to change your mind."

"I'm sure."

He nodded. He should have been excited. He had just earned his share of the ten thousand that the state was paying for her public defender and he didn't even have to go to trial. But his gut was tight and anxiety ate at him—he didn't want her to take this deal. Who knew how long the parole board would keep her? And once she was out, she would be a convicted felon.

"I'll set up a meeting with the prosecutor," he said. "Do you need anything?"

She smiled. "You're sweet. No, but thanks."

Brigham rose. He watched as a guard took her arm and helped her out of the room. He could see into the cell block. Inmates were stacked on top of each other like chickens in a coop. A few of them were sleeping, some watching television. One woman looked at him and pulled up her shirt, exposing her breasts, before the metal door slid shut.

Thirteen

Another late night of reading and research, and Brigham's nerves were on edge from all the coffee he was drinking. He decided he needed a break. He went out to a gas station nearby and got bottled water and a sandwich.

Back at the office, he ate in the library as he read. Case law in Utah was notoriously sparse. Not much happened here that was worth the review of the Supreme Court, particularly in criminal cases.

A few cases discussed mental health defenses against homicide. Molly had been right—the standard was that the defendant didn't understand the nature of what they were doing because of some sort of permanent or temporary mental dysfunction. The defense would have to show that the defendant didn't know the difference between right and wrong, then they'd need to have a psychiatrist testify that the defendant didn't understand this as a direct result of their mental illness or dysfunction. It seemed like an impossible standard to meet.

"Haven't seen anyone read like that since law school."

Tommy came and sat across from him. He lit a cigar and put a foot up on the table. Brigham guessed Tommy's Italian leather shoes cost more than his own apartment's rent for a year.

"We're gonna try for manslaughter," Brigham said.

"You don't sound too enthusiastic."

"I don't know if she should get that."

"Why?"

"Doesn't seem fair. The guy killed her daughter. Who wouldn't do what she did?"

"A lotta people." He puffed out some smoke and then held the cigar low between two fingers. "What do you think justice is, Brigham?"

"I don't know."

"Nobody does. It's all a guess. It may not even exist. But if it does, getting what you deserve is about as close to it as I can estimate. So you can't think about justice. You'll go crazy with how much injustice there is. You just gotta do your job and do whatever the client wants. Does she want to take manslaughter?"

"Yeah."

"Well, your job isn't to contradict her wishes." He raised the cigar and took a few puffs. "Then again, some of our clients are stupider than a dim-witted cow. You gotta do what's good for 'em 'cause they won't."

Tommy rose and placed his hand on Brigham's shoulder. "You'll get it done. Either way."

———

Brigham researched every possible case similar to his that Utah had ever had, which wasn't as many as he had hoped. The sun was coming up by the time he was through. Every muscle ached and his vision was blurry. He had stopped drinking coffee. For the first time, he realized his hands were trembling and he was getting a headache.

When he went home, his door was open a crack. He was always careful about locking it and would sometimes check it three or four times. Someone had been in there.

He opened the door wide and looked inside. His futon cushion had been thrown on the floor. His small television was off-kilter, and several drawers in the kitchen were open. Twisting the doorknob, he saw that the lock had been bashed in.

Moving quickly, he went through the apartment. The only thing he noticed missing was a pair of sneakers he'd had in the closet. Out of everything in his apartment, the only thing of worth they could find was a pair of old sneakers. He couldn't tell whether that made him happy or depressed.

Forgoing calling the police, he woke the landlord instead and asked for a new lock before collapsing into bed.

When he woke, it was after midday. His head was pounding in a full-out migraine and pain shot through the left side of his back. He stood up and tried to stretch before he noticed he had a message on his phone. It was from Molly, letting him know that she had called the prosecutor and they had an appointment set for three o'clock this afternoon to see if they could resolve the case. The clock on his phone said it was 2:24.

Brigham jumped into the shower and out again a few minutes later, threw on his suit, and ran a brush through his hair. He was out the door and on his bike before he remembered he couldn't lock his door. He ran back inside. In the air vent in the bathroom was a wad of cash, his emergency stash to buy food or pay rent if he ever ran out of money. He stuffed it into his sock and headed back out toward the district attorney's office downtown.

Fourteen

The DA's office was in a tall glass-and-chrome building across the street from a Thai food restaurant and a gym. Kitty-corner from it was another office building filled with law firms and stock brokerages. Brigham rushed into the building. He'd gotten there with three minutes to spare. Molly was sitting in a lounge chair doing something on her phone. She saw him and rose.

"Cutting it close."

"Sorry. My apartment was burglarized."

"Seriously?"

"They only took some old sneakers. Not a big deal."

They strolled to the elevators and pressed the button. "You seem pretty calm."

"What's done is done. Besides, if they're willing to break into an apartment to steal some shoes, they needed them more than I did."

Molly pressed the button to the sixth floor and Brigham checked his hair in the mirror on the ceiling of the elevator. His top button was loose so he buttoned it and redid his tie.

The DA's office took up three floors. Brigham hung back as Molly talked to the receptionist, who hurried off, then returned and told them that they were free to go back. They passed through metal detectors, and a security guard double-checked Brigham with a wand for a minute before letting him through.

Assistant District Attorney Vince Dale had the large corner office. Molly entered first.

"Vince, how are you?"

"Good, babe. How are you?"

"Not bad."

She sat down and Brigham followed suit. Vince's desk was huge, too large to reach across and shake hands. He was chewing gum loudly and popped it. His suit was immaculate and his shirt and bow tie combination could have come from the pages of *GQ*. His hair was slicked back and the watch on his wrist glimmered in the sunlight coming through the windows.

"So you must be Brigham," he said.

"Yes, sir."

"Well, Brigham, you're in the big leagues now. How does it feel?"

"It's fine, sir."

Vince grinned and they stared at each other a moment. "Well, I'll teach you the ropes. See, ask Molly here or your boss Tommy— I don't file capital cases unless I'm gonna get a conviction. You understand? If there's any chance of me losing, I wouldn't file it."

"I understand."

"Good. Just so we're both on the same page. Now, what is it I can do for you?"

Molly said, "We've reviewed the evidence. Given the mitigating circumstances, we were hoping you'd be willing to offer manslaughter."

"Hm. I had thought about that. But babe, I just don't see why I should. I got her cold. I could get a conviction in my sleep. So I don't see why she should get a slap on the wrist for killing a man."

"That man," Brigham said, "raped and killed her six-year-old daughter."

71

"It's not her place to determine what happens to him." His head tilted oddly to the side, a glimmer in his eye as he said, "It's mine. So she can plead to agg murder, and I won't seek the death penalty."

"We'll take manslaughter," Brigham said. "Nothing else."

Vince made a clicking sound through his teeth. "See, now you're new at this so I'll try and educate you some, son. I could have her killed. I'm offering not to have her killed. So you just gotta ask your client, 'Do you want to live, or don't you?'"

Brigham rose. "It was nice meeting you."

Vince leaned back in his seat, one leg coming over the other. "You're a fiery little bastard, aren't you?"

Brigham strode out of the office, leaving the door open behind him. Molly followed. They didn't speak until they were by the elevators.

"He's trying to help," she said.

"He's a prick."

"He's offering to spare her life. That's not worthless. You need to calm down and look at this case objectively."

Brigham shook his head as he stepped on the elevator. "He doesn't give a shit about her."

She sighed. "No, he doesn't. But it's not his job to care. It's ours."

"I'm going to tell her not to take it."

"That's not up to you, Brigham. You take her the offer and let her make up her own mind. Life in prison, or death at the hands of the state."

"She doesn't deserve this, Molly."

"*Deserve* has nothing to do with the law. You can't think like that."

He shook his head again. The elevator doors opened and he stepped out and headed for the front doors. By the time he was standing on the sidewalk, he had calmed down and felt stupid for showing his anger in front of Molly and Vince.

In law school, when he pictured himself as a lawyer, he always saw himself as cool and collected. The type of lawyer that judges would value input from, because they knew it came from an objective person. Now he felt like a child, throwing a tantrum because he wasn't getting his way.

"Sorry," he said.

"It's all right. I can tell this is important to you. But this is your first big case. You'll have dozens of others in your career. Are you going to storm out of every prosecutor's office when they don't see a case your way?"

"She . . ."

"I know. But you're going to work with Vince again. A lot. He's probably going to be the next DA. You need a good working relationship with him. Never blow your relationship with a prosecutor over one case."

He nodded. "I better go. I wanna get the offer to her before dinner."

On his third visit to the jail, Brigham began noticing the little things—the grinding sound the door made when it slid open, the way the gray paint on the cement floors was peeling off, how dirty the glass partitions, separating visitors from inmates, were.

This time, he was the first one in the cell block, and waited for the guard to bring Amanda out. When she came in, she smiled at him while looking him in the eyes: a first. She sat across from him and he smiled back.

"Are you doing okay?"

She nodded. "I'm okay. They have some classes here through the community college. I've been taking some. It keeps me busy."

"Well, that's good. Stay as busy as you can." He glanced down to a fingerprint smear on his side of the glass. It was about the size of a child's. "I'm obligated to relay to you any offers made by the prosecution. The lead prosecutor on this case offered to remove the death penalty option if you plead guilty to homicide. You would get life in prison instead—fifteen to life."

The smile faded from her face. She looked like someone had just punched her in the gut and all the wind had left her.

"Fifteen to life?" she repeated.

"Yes. I'm sorry."

She was silent a moment. "What do you think I should do?"

"I think . . . I think you should fight it. The chances of us winning are slim. If we lose, there is a very real possibility that you could be sentenced to death. The way it works is, after you're convicted of homicide, the jury would then have to decide if you should get the death penalty. It's like another trial. But no woman has ever been executed in Utah. I think the prosecutor is bluffing."

"But I killed him. How can we win?"

"It's a specialized defense. We're going to say you were so distraught that it caused a type of temporary insanity. It would negate the intent of this crime."

She stared down at the metal counter in front of her, running her finger along the corner where it met the glass. The muscles in her jaw flexed. "I'll do whatever you tell me to do."

They held each other's gaze a moment, and then she rose without a word and left him alone again, staring at his reflection in the glass.

Fifteen

Brigham stopped at the office that night but had so little energy, he couldn't bring himself to open another book in the library. Scotty was still working and asked a quick question about criminal restitution: whether a store could sue someone and ask for criminal restitution if the person shoplifted something. Brigham looked up the answer for him in Lexis and then left.

The night was much colder than the day had led him to expect it would be. Riding his bike, the frosty air stung his cheeks and made his nose run. He got to his apartment and noticed a familiar car parked by the curb. Molly was sitting in the driver's seat. She stepped out with a six-pack of Heineken in her hand.

"Thought you could use some company," she said.

"I can. My apartment isn't much."

"I'm fine with it, Brigham. No need to show how macho and rich you are."

He grinned as he walked his bike inside and held the door open for her. Somebody's front door suddenly opened. June stood there, a surprised look on her face when she saw Molly.

"Hey," she said.

"Hey," Brigham replied. "Molly, this is June."

June said, "Call me later."

She went back inside and closed the door, leaving Brigham wondering what had just happened.

Brigham took Molly down the steps to his apartment. He watched her face, but there was no reaction of disgust. In fact, she flopped on the couch and opened a beer like she had been coming there for months.

"So, not to talk about work," she said, "but did you visit her?"

Brigham walked into the kitchen to get two glasses and some ice. "Yeah."

"And?"

"She says she'll do whatever I want her to do."

"Seriously? She barely knows you. Must just have that kind of face."

He came back and placed the glasses down on the worn coffee table he'd bought at a garage sale. The remote was still there—the burglars hadn't taken that—and he flipped on the television, which had a crack in the center of the screen.

"What're you going to tell her?" she asked.

He poured the beer in a glass half-filled with ice and took a sip. "I don't know."

"Beer with ice, huh?"

"I can't drink warm beer," he said. "Reminds me of this time when I was a kid and I drank my own piss on a dare."

"Ech. Must've been some dare."

"Not really. I didn't even like the kid or care what he thought about me. I just didn't like that he thought I couldn't do it."

She shook her head as she stared at the television. "Little boys are so weird."

He leaned back on the beanbag he had in place of a chair and brought the glass to his lips. The beer was still lukewarm, and he felt like gagging. "So what should I tell her?"

"Tell her to take the deal and save her life."

The television flipped to a game show. He and his neighbor had the same type of remote and they occasionally crossed signals.

"I don't want to tell her that."

"This isn't about what you want. It's about what's best for your client. You always have to remember that. It's about them. You're not the one that has to live with the repercussions."

He exhaled and then took another drink. "I didn't think being a lawyer would be like this. When I was interning with the public defenders, it was all DUIs and drug charges. You'd get them a fine and some classes and move on to the next case."

"I was a corporate lawyer at my first job. Our firm's business was sixty percent from one client. We just had to do whatever the client wanted. No gray areas, no soul searching. I thought all law practice was like that—you'd look up a case or a statute and it'd have all the answers you were looking for. But when you deal with people instead of corporations, it's not like that."

"Why'd you leave?"

"The firm?" she replied.

"Yeah. You must've been pulling down some serious cash."

"One eighty a year."

He whistled. "It'd take a lot for me to leave a paycheck like that. More than getting groped by a few bosses."

"I saw the people who had been there for ten or twenty years. On their third marriages, bogged down with fancy cars and jewelry to show each other how much money they make . . . and the worst part was that they lived there. They didn't even have the chance to really enjoy their money. Their vacations were always filled with work, so they started going places they couldn't be reached, like jungles and mountains. They were miserable and they couldn't face it. I didn't want that life."

"So how'd you meet Tommy?"

She sipped her beer out of the bottle, foregoing the ice. "I went up against him in a divorce case. I liked him. He was gaudy; don't get me wrong. But he was unique. We had lunch, and he told me that if I was ever sick of working for assholes I should come work with him. One day, I just took him up on it." She paused. "What about you?"

"I needed a job."

"You'd eventually find something if you kept trying."

He shrugged. "I liked him, too."

She finished her beer in a few gulps and rose. "You better get to bed. Tomorrow's her arraignment. You know where the Matheson Courthouse is?"

"Yeah."

"Don't be late. Judge Ganche, eight thirty."

She took another beer from the six-pack on her way out. As she was leaving, she tapped it against his glass. "To living in the gray."

Brigham watched her go. As she turned toward her car, she glanced back at him. The television switched to an adult channel and began ordering a porno.

"Jim?" Brigham shouted.

"Yeah, man," a voice came from next door.

"I can see your porn."

"Cool, man. You wanna pay for half, then?"

Sixteen

The Matheson Courthouse was named after a former US Attorney and current federal judge for the Tenth Circuit Court of Appeals. It was rumored he had never actually seen it.

The building was square and consisted of blue glass with a few white pillars thrown in to remind people it was actually a court.

Brigham waited in line at the metal detectors. He looked at the fresco on the ceiling five stories above him, but he couldn't make out what it was.

The bailiffs made him take off his belt and shoes. He still set off the machine and they checked him with the wand before he could put his belt back on.

The directory past the metal detectors said that Judge Ganche was on the third floor. Brigham took the elevators up with a group of attorneys. They were discussing buying distressed properties from the Catholic Church. Apparently the Church was selling off prime real estate for pennies to pay off all the settlements for sexual abuse at the hands of priests.

The third floor was packed with attorneys and defendants rushing to courtrooms and the clerk's office. Judge Ganche's room was down the west hallway, and a group of defendants were sitting outside on benches. The courtroom was overflowing; people were lined up outside the door. Brigham slipped between them, muttering, "Excuse me," several times before he actually made it in.

The courtroom was windowless, as most were, and cold. He walked to the front. A line of attorneys sat there. The three prosecutors had stacks of files on the table in front of them, in alphabetical order. Vince wasn't there.

Brigham got in line. Molly came in a few minutes later. She stood next to him. "Hey."

"Hey," he whispered.

"So address bail, but I don't think Ganche is going to release."

"How much is reasonable?"

"She killed a man in front of witnesses and didn't care. I don't think any amount is reasonable, so you might as well go for broke and ask for her to be released on her own recognizance."

The bailiff bellowed, "All rise. Third District Court is now in session. The Honorable Thomas Ganche now presiding."

"Be seated," the judge said.

He was an older man, perhaps sixty-five or sixty-six, and had a droopy, bloodhound face. He looked unhappy to be there and his position meant he didn't have to hide it.

"Any private counsel ready to go?"

An attorney jumped up, cutting off an older woman who needed help getting to her feet. He called his case as the woman glared at him from behind.

Brigham didn't want to cut anybody off and he didn't want to fight with old ladies, so he waited. Besides, he had nowhere else to be.

When his turn did come, he meandered to the podium. This courtroom was much larger than the ones he'd been in before. At least a hundred people were packed in like sardines. Suddenly he felt nervous, and his voice cracked when he said, "The matter of Amanda Pierce, please, Your Honor."

The bailiff opened the door to the holding cells and shouted, "Pierce, you're up."

Another bailiff escorted her out. She was in her orange jumpsuit with a white laceless slipper. Thick handcuffs around her wrists were linked by a chain to her one ankle. The chains rattled as she walked with her crutch, and were so large that they looked like they could slip off her hands at any second. She gave him a melancholy smile and then faced the judge.

"We'd like to enter 'not guilty' pleas, Your Honor."

The judge scowled at him. "First state your appearance."

"Oh, sorry. Brigham Theodore for the defense."

"Rob Heil for the state, filling in for Mr. Dale."

The judge quickly flipped through a file. "Mr. Theodore, this is a felony. You don't need to plead not guilty, it's just assumed it's not guilty and we set it out for another date."

Brigham cleared his throat. He needed to take some action, make some movement, and couldn't think of anything else to do. "Yes, Your Honor. Just wanted to be clear. I would like to address bail, however."

"So address it."

Brigham took out his phone and glanced at the bullet-point list he'd made and read over twenty times. He had it memorized, but now couldn't remember a single item on it.

The only two things the judge looked at in setting bail were flight risk and a threat to the community. If the defendants were at risk of driving to Mexico, the judge would keep them. And if they were going to go out and hurt somebody while released, he'd keep them as well.

Years ago when Brigham had first learned that, it had shocked him to his core. What it said essentially was that the government didn't need to convict a person of a crime to lock someone up and ruin the person's life. All they needed to do was accuse that person.

And if accused of something serious enough, they would lock the person up until it was resolved. Even if found innocent later, the person could easily have served a year or two in jail already.

"Your Honor, Ms. Pierce is a veteran with no criminal history. She has ties to the community through her work and her church and has never done anything to make this court think that she is a flight risk. She doesn't even have a passport or a car anymore. As far as threat to the community, this was an isolated incident, something that could only have affected one person, and that person is no longer with us. She had a disposition to—"

"Bail is denied, Counsel."

"Your Honor, if I might be heard, I'd like to point out that—"

"She killed someone in broad daylight. Sorry, but I'm not letting her roam free. Bail denied. I'm guessing you want a roll call hearing, right?"

"Um, Your Honor, I would like to finish addressing bail."

"Counsel approach, please." The judge pressed a button on his bench that made static noise play through the speakers so no one in the courtroom could hear what they were talking about. Ganche waited until both Brigham and the prosecutor stood in front of him.

"Mr. Theodore," the judge whispered, "you're new, so I'm going to take it easy on you. But once I've made my ruling, I've made my ruling. You don't question me. I am the law in here. Do you understand?"

"She shouldn't be locked up, Your Honor. She's not a threat to anybody."

"I think she is. And what I think is more important than what you think."

"What happened to innocent until proven guilty?"

The judge smirked. "A wet dream Jefferson had. Now get back to the podium."

Brigham walked back and stood there as the judge's clerk searched for a date for the roll call. His anxiety and nervousness had turned to anger. He wanted to lash out at the judge, but he looked over at Molly. She moved her palm down, reminding him to calm down.

"Two weeks from today," the judge said. "Make sure Mr. Dale is here so we can settle this, Mr. Heil."

Brigham put his arm on Amanda's shoulder. "I'll come visit you soon."

He watched as the bailiff pulled her back into the holding cells, and the door slammed shut.

Seventeen

The weather had turned from rainy and gray to sunny and cloudless in an instant. Brigham sat in his office reading a law review article from the University of Texas describing the standard of proof in mental health defenses. Scotty shuffled in. He paused in the doorway, but changed his mind and left. Then he stopped in the hallway, mumbled to himself, and came and sat down across from Brigham.

"What's up, Scotty?"

"This case makes me nervous."

"What case?"

"Amanda Pierce."

"Why does it make you nervous?"

"'Cause you seem like a nice kid. I've seen a bunch of lawyers grow bitter because of what happens in court. I just don't want that to happen to you."

Brigham couldn't help but grin. Scotty's concern seemed genuine and it wasn't a trait he'd seen in many law students or attorneys. "I'll be okay."

Scotty nodded sadly and rose, wringing his hands as he trudged back to his office.

Molly came in after that and sat down without a word. She ran her finger along the edge of the desk, wiping off some debris that had fallen from the wood-paneled ceilings. Brigham put the law review article down and looked at her.

"What?" she said.

"I think you're starting to care about this case."

"There's nothing wrong with hating to lose."

"There's nothing wrong with caring about a case, either."

She looked out the window. A car was parking and a man in a suit got out, wiping his nose. A woman stumbled out of the passenger seat in a nearly see-through dress. "I have to admit, this is more interesting than divorce cases. You have someone's life on the line."

Brigham watched her. The way the ends of her hair rested on her shoulders. The perfect outline of her face, her hands with the slender fingers that ended in brightly colored nails.

"I'd like to take you to dinner and a movie tonight," he said.

"Like a date?"

"Not *like* a date. *A* date."

"That's pretty forward of you."

"I've been practicing in the mirror."

She chuckled. "I can see it . . . okay, yeah. Dinner and a movie. But I'm paying. I'm not having you miss your rent because you took me out."

"I'm secure enough in my masculinity to accept that."

"Tonight then. After work."

Her phone buzzed and she rose, answering it as she walked out. Brigham went back to his article but couldn't concentrate. Excitement tingled in his belly. He finally put the article away and decided he needed to be somewhere else. The coffee shop seemed as good a place as any. He strolled over there casually and found a seat near the entrance.

He checked Facebook, something he hadn't done for at least a month. Old friends from back home were posting photos of their children. He flipped through, a smile on his face as he watched a video of a young boy trying to get the family dog out of his bed. He'd always figured twenty-six was too young for children and marriage, but now he wondered if he'd missed something, if that age—the age where you're dirt poor and have to scrape together enough to eat every night—built some sort of bond in the marriage that was required to last long-term. Everyone he knew who had married later in life got divorced.

"Brigham?"

A man with brown hair and glasses stood in front of him, a Columbia coat wrapped tightly around him though it wasn't that cold. The man had studied with Brigham at the library for the Bar, along with probably a dozen other graduating law students.

"Terrance, what's up, man?"

Terrance sat down, removing the backpack that hung from his shoulder. "Haven't seen you since the internship," Terrance said. "How you been?"

"Good. Did they finally offer you a position?"

"No, unfortunately. The public defenders are usually the first thing cut in a budget crisis. They said they'd keep my résumé for whenever a position opened up, though."

"Seems like a fun place to work."

Terrance grinned. "Better than clerkships and big firms, man. I never wanted to go that route."

Brigham noticed a ring on Terrance's finger. "Are you married?"

Terrance held up his hand, displaying the ring fully. "Yup. Two weeks ago. Can't afford a honeymoon yet, but hopefully soon."

"Your wife's cool with that?"

He shrugged. "What can she do? We don't have the money. And our parents aren't helping us. So where you working nowadays?"

"Law Office of TTB."

"Haven't heard of them. What type of law?"

"Criminal defense."

"Seriously? Good for you."

"It's nothing serious. I get a cut of any cases I work. No salary or benefits."

"Better than nothing, which is what I got right now. I might have to fall back on my computer science degree and get another programming job. That's what I was doing right before law school put me eighty grand in debt. I think law was a bad decision."

"Too late now."

Terrance smirked as he glimpsed a couple coming inside the coffee shop. "Ain't that the truth." He stood. "It was nice seeing you. Stay in touch."

"I will. You on Facebook?"

"I am. Look me up."

Brigham surfed the Internet another few minutes before a smell caught his attention. He saw someone with a panini and a bag of chips. He pulled out his wallet. Exactly two dollars.

Brigham bought a bag of chips for a dollar seventy-five and left the quarter change in the tip jar. He ate slowly by the window, hoping to drag out the snack to make his brain think he was fuller than he was. A light drizzle of rain began. It pelted the window and his reflection looked speckled. The streets were quickly gleaming wet.

Across the street near the Trax station, an officer sprinted after a man trying to flee. The officer tackled him at the waist and two more police cruisers pulled up. Brigham pictured the man in jail and then in court. He saw the officers testifying about what happened, embellishing the man's attempt to flee. He saw himself in court, trying to fight for him in a system where fairness had no place.

What the hell have I gotten myself into?

The first date came quickly. Brigham stood in front of his bathroom mirror and stared at every hair to make sure it was in the right place. His best shirt, a blue polo shirt he'd gotten at a secondhand store, looked about two years past its prime. He flipped the collar up, decided he looked like a frat boy, and then folded it down. Then he tried it with a jacket, then with a baseball cap. Eventually, he decided the best policy was to be himself. Molly was clearly out of his league, and there was no way there was going to be a second date so he might as well relax and have fun. He left the shirt on but took off the slacks and put on jeans and sneakers.

She picked him up and he felt elated in a way he could only describe to himself as giddy. Then he felt stupid for being almost thirty and feeling giddy, and tried to play it cool. Which, of course, backfired when he brought up *Battlestar Galactica* on the drive to the restaurant and Molly looked at him like he was crazy.

The dinner was in a trendy Italian restaurant. Boccio's. The lights glimmered like gems in the dark as they strolled inside, a doorman holding the door open. The doorman looked to Molly, who wore a beautiful gown, and then his brow furrowed when he looked to Brigham.

I know, Brigham thought.

Brigham felt awkward there among people for whom money was just a given, like air. He had a deep sense that they were different than him. Not better, but different.

"You don't go on many dates, do you?" Molly said between the main course and dessert.

"That obvious?"

"I don't either."

"Really? You seem like a pro. I don't mean pro, I mean . . . I don't think you're a hooker, I meant . . . I'm going to go ahead and be quiet now."

She chuckled, and Brigham thought making her laugh had to be the best feeling he'd ever had.

"You're adorable when you're flustered," she said.

After dinner, Brigham insisted on paying but Molly took the check. "You buy the ice cream," she said.

A sense of relief washed over Brigham. Though he had planned on paying, the check was more than he spent on groceries in a month.

The two of them strolled downtown. Though Utah had a reputation as being conservative, downtown Salt Lake City at night was always packed with crowds rushing into the various bars and clubs, art shows, and improv theaters.

"Why Salt Lake?" he said, as his hands went inside his pockets and Molly hooked her arm in his.

"It's slow. People are more friendly here than in California. Less stress, I guess. That's the great destroyer of civilizations now. Stress." She paused. "You don't seem that stressed to me."

"Maybe I just shove it way down where I don't think it'll affect me." He looked to her. "Until I blow up and jump off a bridge, I guess."

She smiled. "Well, don't jump just yet. I'm actually having fun."

Molly leaned in and kissed him. The kiss was light, a peck, but his lips seemed to buzz afterward. As though the touch rejuvenated him. A sense came over him that Molly could have asked him to do just about anything for her right now and he would've done it. But all she did was rest her head on his shoulder as they walked the clean sidewalks, and gaze at the stars in the clear sky on the way to an ice cream parlor up the street.

Eighteen

Two weeks came and went in the blink of an eye. Brigham's days were spent researching motions and drafting cross-examinations for the eventual preliminary hearing and trial. He used Scotty as his mock jury, but he frequently fell asleep because of an anti-anxiety medication he was on. Brigham let him sleep and kept going.

The roll call was as packed as the arraignment. Brigham came early to the courthouse so he could get the first spot. He went into the holding cells and sat in a chair in the corner. A bailiff shouted, "Pierce. Your lawyer's back here."

Amanda quietly walked out with a rattle from the chains. She sat across from him and tried to smile. She looked pale and skinny.

"Everything all right at the jail?" he asked.

"Fine."

"They're feeding you okay and everything?"

She shrugged. "It doesn't matter."

"If you're having any problems, let me know."

She looked up at him. "I'm fine. What're we doing today?"

"We're just going to be setting the case for what's called a preliminary hearing. It's kind of like a miniature trial. The state has to present enough evidence to convince a judge that a crime was committed and that you committed it. They have to show evidence for every element of every crime they're charging you with. But the standard is much lower than a trial. Just enough to make sure they have the right person."

She nodded. "Okay."

"Do you have any questions?"

"No."

"Okay, I'll call your case as soon as I can."

Brigham hurried back to the courtroom. At least five lawyers were now ahead of him. As he went to sit down at the end of the bench, the doors to the courtroom opened and Vince Dale walked in.

The suit he was wearing probably cost more than anyone else's in the courtroom. The knot of his bow tie today was perfectly flawed, just enough to show that it wasn't a cheap pre-tied one. His pocket square echoed a glimpse of the lining of his suit. An assistant trailed behind him, holding his files and a laptop. Brigham had asked Tommy about Vince, and all Tommy had said was that Vince Dale was next in line to be district attorney. He had the political support of the county Republican Party, which was essentially a guarantee that he would be DA, and he had wealthy backers. Brigham wondered how it was someone found wealthy backers—probably with deals they wouldn't want made public.

"Mr. Theodore," Vince said, a smile on his lips. "So glad you could make it."

"We'll still take manslaughter if you wanna offer it."

He scoffed. "I think we're past the point of negotiation." "Guess you're right. Conviction in a big case like this right before an election looks pretty good, don't it?"

Vince leaned down, close enough to whisper. "I eat cocky assholes like you for breakfast."

Brigham grinned. "Yeah, that's the kind of breakfast I'd expect of you." He leaned back. "Might want to get comfortable. I'm last in line."

"Nonsense. Now we can't have poor Ms. Pierce sitting on pins and needles, can we?" Vince went up to the podium, practically pushing a female defense attorney out of the way, and said to the bailiff, "I'm ready on my case."

The bailiff, as if receiving an order from his boss, went back behind the judge's seat and through a door. He came back out a minute later and said, "All rise. Third District Court is now in session. The Honorable Thomas Ganche presiding."

The judge sat down and turned on his computer before noticing Vince.

"Mr. Dale, pleasure to see you again."

"You too, Your Honor. How was George's graduation?"

"Four grandchildren down and two to go. Then I can retire once they're all out of college."

"Well, that would certainly be our loss."

He grinned as the clerk handed him a red file. "Opinions vary on that, I think. What have you got today?"

"Amanda Pierce, Your Honor."

Ganche scanned the courtroom and his eyes rested on Brigham. "Care to join us, Mr. Theodore?"

Brigham confidently strode to the defense podium to the sneers of a few defense attorneys. It reminded him of a group of vultures laughing at one of their own who was about to be eaten.

"What's anticipated, Counsel?"

Brigham said, "We request a preliminary hearing, Your Honor."

Ganche looked at both of them and then closed the file. "In chambers, please."

Vince strolled around the podium and casually walked across the courtroom, following the judge through the door that the bailiff had used earlier. Brigham followed.

That was how powerful judges were, Brigham thought. That they could leave a hundred people at any time and the people would just have to wait for them.

They went back to the judge's chambers, nothing but a large office with its own bathroom. An American flag hung on one wall, along with several photos of a young Thomas Ganche in military uniform. His diplomas, displayed prominently behind the desk where everyone entering could see them, said he received his undergraduate degree from Cornell and his law degree from the University of Texas.

"Don't tell me you have your eyes on a trial," he said.

Vince went to a mini-fridge and took a bottle of water. He sat down next to Brigham and unbuttoned his suit coat.

"Yes, we are going to trial," Brigham said.

Ganche shook his head. "Son, that is just stupid. What's the offer?"

"Homicide, fifteen to life," Vince said.

Ganche turned to Brigham. "No death penalty. That's a fine offer for something done with people around."

"I'll decide after prelim," Brigham insisted.

Vince took a sip of the water. "After prelim, the offer's off the table."

"Why?"

"Because you're going to make me do a prelim on a case that you should plead to."

Ganche shrugged in an up-to-you way.

"I'll talk to my client," Brigham said.

"You do that," Ganche said. "We'll wait."

Brigham hesitated and then rose. He went out to the courtroom and to Amanda, who was still standing at the podium.

"The prosecutor said if you don't take the deal right now, it's off the table."

"I have to decide right now?" she asked.

"I'm afraid so."

She thought for a second. "What do you think?"

"I think we should tell them to shove their deal where the sun don't shine. But if we lose, I'm not the one that's looking at the death penalty."

She shook her head. "They just want me to go away. I saw my case in the news. They want me to go away."

"Maybe. It can't look good to parents that someone who did what you did is facing the death penalty. You'd also be the first woman to face it in this state. I don't think the prosecutor wants to be known as the first prosecutor in Utah to execute a woman."

She nodded. "I want to fight it."

"Are you sure? There's no going back after today."

"I'm sure."

He glanced to another inmate, who was drooling and staring blankly at the wall. "I will do everything I can to take care of you."

"I know you will."

Brigham went back into the judge's chambers. Ganche and Vince were laughing about something. They stopped when he came in. Brigham didn't sit this time.

"My client has turned down the offer. We'll be moving forward."

The judge sighed. "It's a mistake, son. She'll die."

"All of us in here know the state of Utah isn't going to execute a woman. Especially one that killed a homicidal rapist pedophile. So both of you can stop trying to intimidate me."

"I would watch your tone, young man," the judge warned. "You need to respect this Court as you would respect the law itself."

"Respect the law?"

"Counsel, you better—"

"If I sense that you are not being fair, totally fair, for even a second, I will file a motion to recuse you. I'm sure you don't want to be recused from a case that's getting national press any more than Vince does."

Brigham paused to see the effect of his words on both men. Vince was grinning, but the judge's face was twisted in anger and slightly blushing.

Brigham turned and walked out. His heart was thumping as if it were trying to break out of his chest and fly away.

Nineteen

The preliminary hearing was set on a Wednesday morning. On the Tuesday morning before, Brigham was in his office reading transcripts of murder trials where the defense had obtained an acquittal. Every single one had the exact same strategy: paint the victim as the biggest lowlife in the world. Make it seem like the defendant had done the world a favor by offing the victim. In this case, it wouldn't be difficult to do.

Tommy walked in with an unlit cigar dangling from his mouth. He placed a check on the desk and slid it toward Brigham. The check was for $4500.

"What is this?"

"For you. The murder."

"It's more than a quarter."

"I know. You've earned it. And when you get to trial, I'm going to let you keep the full thing."

Brigham stared at the check. He had never seen one for this amount. "I'm fine with the deal. You don't have to do this, Tommy."

"I know I don't have to. I want to. You're doing good work. Besides, Law Offices of TTB is in the news every week. You can't buy that kind of advertising."

He turned and left, leaving Brigham staring at the check. $4500. Enough to pay rent for a year, or buy groceries for just as long. He could stretch this money out for a long time. He placed the check in his bag and went back to the transcripts.

Over the past two weeks, he and Molly had been spending the evenings together.

After the first couple of dates, their initial format of dinner and a movie had turned into drinks at her place. Now, he was over there almost every night.

She lived in a high-rise downtown that Brigham didn't think he would ever be able to afford. The condo overlooked the entire city and had white carpets with mirrored walls. More than once, Brigham had fallen asleep in the hot tub next to the pool on her roof while reading legal treatises on Molly's iPad. Her soft touch would wake him and they'd go downstairs to her bedroom.

Brigham had always felt somewhat awkward in the bedroom, but Molly knew exactly what to do. She was perfect in the nude, an image of feminine beauty. Even the way she smelled drove him crazy, and he found himself thinking about her when he wasn't with her.

One night, when they were lying in her bed with moonlight cascading over them, she told him that she hadn't been with a man in a long time—not since her messy divorce complete with all the clichés, including an insane husband who used to beat her in drunken rages, an affair, and a nasty financial split, which all culminated in her leaving her hometown of Los Angeles and moving to Salt Lake City, of all places.

Brigham listened quietly. He could tell this was something she hadn't intended to share with anyone, so he didn't say anything. He just held her and they watched the moon out the windows.

The next morning, he felt a bond to her that he knew hadn't been there the night before. She had shown him a wound she didn't want seen and it was a secret between them now. Secrets had the power to make people stick together against the rest of the world.

On the morning of the preliminary hearing, Brigham had a breakfast of Cap'n Crunch and rode his bike straight to the courthouse. The bailiff had now seen him on three separate occasions and still got out his wand for him.

In the courtroom he waited a good half hour while the judge took care of some housekeeping matters: two cases that had motions for him to sign. Then the judge called Amanda Pierce.

Tommy had told Brigham that the preliminary hearing was the most important hearing in a criminal case—what the state or the defense thought a witness was going to say was almost never what they were actually going to say, and prelim was the place to discover that. It was held in front of a different judge than that assigned to the trial, so the trial judge wouldn't know the case before the trial.

Today's judge was an older woman with white hair. Her face looked carved of stone: no emotion whatsoever. Her voice was deadpan. Even when she was sentencing the defendant of the case before to jail, she sounded like she was reading a phone book.

The Court had to wait ten minutes for Vince Dale to show up. The judge didn't say anything as he and his assistant set up a laptop on the prosecution table. Brigham figured that if he had been the one who was ten minutes late, he'd probably be in cuffs.

He glanced behind him. Molly was sitting where the defense attorneys usually sat in line. She smiled at him and he couldn't help smiling back. Scotty sat next to her, nodding off.

"Your Honor," Vince said, "the state is ready to proceed with the Amanda Pierce preliminary hearing."

The bailiff brought Amanda out to sit next to Brigham. He had several legal pads in front of him, and on his laptop were the cross-examination questions he had prepared for the officers and witnesses.

"Your Honor, the state moves to admit eleven-oh-two statements in lieu of today's witnesses," Vince said.

"Any objection from the defense?"

"Um, one moment, Your Honor." He turned to Molly and leaned close to her ear. "Can he do that?"

"Yes," she whispered. "Eleven-oh-two lets them submit affidavits instead of testimony. But I've never seen a prosecutor do it with all their witnesses. They usually do it with one or two."

Brigham faced the judge. "Your Honor, I would object on the grounds that my client doesn't get an opportunity to confront her accusers."

"This is prelim, I don't believe she has that right here."

"I think if we look at the intent of a preliminary hearing, it is so the client is not wrongly accused of a crime, so that someone can sit on that stand and point the finger and say 'yes, that's her right there.' The state is denying her a preliminary hearing by submitting these documents. How am I supposed to cross-examine documents?"

"Mr. Dale?" the judge said.

"The law is clear, Your Honor," he said, winking at Brigham. "The preliminary hearing is a procedural hearing, not a substantive one. The accused has no right to confront anything. This hearing is strictly for the judge. If the Court feels the affidavits from four sworn law enforcement personnel and three civilian witnesses are inherently trustworthy, that's enough. The accused gets a trial. She doesn't need two."

The judge took a second to think. "That's essentially how I see it, Counsel. I'm allowing the eleven-oh-two statements in lieu of testimony. My clerk will read them into the record."

Brigham sat down as the clerk began reading the statements. They were about as he expected—no one doubted what had happened. Amanda deliberately shot Tyler Moore in the head. The only question in Brigham's mind was whether a jury would convict her for it.

When the clerk had finished reading the last statement, the judge said, "Unless you intend to call the defendant, I'm ready for arguments."

"I'd like to renew my objection," Brigham said, "for the record. And the defendant will not be testifying."

"So noted. Mr. Dale?"

"We'll submit, Your Honor."

The judge began writing on a red file. "I find there is probable cause to bind the defendant over for trial. I'm setting second arraignment out three weeks unless someone has a problem with that. Thank you, Mr. Dale, Counsel."

Amanda turned to Brigham and said, "What does that mean?"

"It means we lost. I'll come visit you soon."

Brigham sat at the defense table as Amanda was taken back to the holding cells. She had a crutch, but every step was a struggle. The bailiff was texting on his phone rather than really helping her.

"It doesn't matter," Molly said behind him. "I've never even *seen* the defense win a prelim and get the case dismissed."

"Why do I get the feeling we're playing a rigged game?"

"Because you are."

Twenty

The days quickly fell into a pattern as the trial approached. The mornings were spent hunting for the perfect expert for Amanda's trial, and the nights were spent at Molly's talking about Amanda's case.

Molly told Brigham several times not to get so attached to one case. If he lost, it would embitter him. But he couldn't help it—the case was the only thing he could think about.

He visited Amanda a couple of times a week, and each time she looked worse. She was losing weight and no longer taking care of herself. She wouldn't talk during their meetings, but instead nodded or shook her head when he asked her something.

Brigham sat in his office a few weeks before the trial. Tommy had given him another case: a misdemeanor DUI. The client had been driving to an AA meeting and stopped at a liquor store on the way. She bought a bottle of whiskey and was drunk by the time she got to the meeting. They called the police before she was even in her seat.

Molly appeared at his door. "Did you hear?"

"Hear what?"

"About Amanda?"

"No, what?"

She hesitated. "Someone tried to kill her in jail."

"How? Is she all right?"

"She's at University Hospital right now."

Brigham jumped up and was out the door. Molly followed behind him, saying, "They're not going to let you see her. Brigham? Brigham . . . well, at least let me drive you."

———

The hospital emergency room had valet parking and, as they rolled to a stop, a man in a red shirt gave them a claim check. Brigham pushed through the revolving doors and up to the front counter. Two receptionists were there doing paperwork.

"I need to see Amanda Pierce, please," he said.

"I'll be with you in a moment, sir."

Brigham paced nervously. Molly had already sat down and was flipping through a magazine. It took nearly ten minutes for the receptionist to say, "Amanda Pierce is a prisoner, sir. She isn't allowed visitors."

"I'm her lawyer."

"I don't care if you're the Pope. No visitors."

Brigham nodded and said, "Let's go, Molly."

As they walked past the double doors leading to the patients' rooms, Brigham glanced back to the receptionist. She'd already returned to whatever paperwork she was doing. A man in scrubs was coming out of the doors. Brigham said, "Wait in the car for me," and pushed through the double doors before Molly could protest.

The linoleum squeaked underneath his shoes as he made his way to the police officer sitting outside a door at the end of the hall. Brigham pulled out his Utah State Bar card and flashed it at the police officer.

"I'm her attorney."

He walked into the room without looking at the officer, as though he'd done it a thousand times and it was routine. His heart was pounding and he wasn't sure he wouldn't be shot. But he made it into the room and shut the door behind him. The officer had stood up and was watching through the glass viewing window on the door.

Amanda looked like a skeleton. Brigham had seen her a few days ago. He wondered if he just hadn't noticed or if she'd really deteriorated in that time. She was in a hospital gown and the side of her neck was bandaged. A dark red stain leaked through the white gauze. Brigham moved closer and sat in a chair next to the bed.

She stirred and her head rolled to the side. Her eyes were red with dark circles below them. Her nostrils flared as if she was having trouble breathing.

"I guess," she rasped, "I just can't stay out of trouble."

"What happened?"

"It's not her fault. She's schizophrenic and shouldn't be in there. She didn't mean to do it."

He shook his head. "It was the woman you were in the holding cells with, wasn't it? I'm going to see if we can have you transferred."

"No. The only place they can transfer me is administrative segregation. I don't want to go there. You're alone twenty-three hours a day."

He exhaled. "I'm so sorry this happened."

Amanda's eyes welled up with tears. Whatever strength she had to hide her emotions from him had faded. She began to sob, and he let her.

"I couldn't save her," she cried. "My baby, my baby . . . That monster tore her apart and I couldn't save her."

Brigham put his hand over hers and let her cry.

Twenty-one

The University of Utah was nearly empty at this time of night. Brigham sat on the lawn of the law school. It was a place he'd come many times when he'd been studying for the Bar exam. When the stress got to be too much, he'd come there and stare at the traffic. Usually, he didn't have the money for booze. But now he'd brought along a bottle of schnapps and he sipped at it as he watched the passing traffic.

Amanda Pierce was probably going to die. If not by the state, then in prison. It wasn't that she was soft, but that she had given up.

Molly texted and asked where he was, and he told her. Within fifteen minutes, she had parked on the street and walked up the lawn. She sat down without saying anything and took a sip of his schnapps.

"I used to sit here and dream about what being a lawyer was like," he said. "I thought it'd be so glamorous. That I'd be pounding a table for my clients and screaming about injustice." He took a long drink. "But injustice is all it is. There's nothing to scream about because there is nothing else."

"That's not true."

"They don't need a conviction—they've already ruined her life. She won't have a job when she gets out, she's lost her house . . . she's lost her daughter. She's down, and the government just won't stop kicking."

Molly placed her hand on his arm. "Then change that. Don't let Vince get a victory because you laid down and felt sorry for yourself. And this is your first big case, Brigham. There'll be other ones where justice does win out. In the end, I think it has to win out."

Brigham took another swig and handed the bottle to her. "If I go down, I'll go down swinging. But I'm not sure it matters in the end."

She placed her fingers lightly on his chin and turned him toward her. "That's all that matters—how well you can walk through flames."

They kissed, and then rose and walked to her car.

The next day, Brigham met with the expert who had gone in to do an evaluation of Amanda. He'd gone through two dozen résumés to find her. She was overly qualified and personable. A jury, he guessed, would like her and be impressed by her.

The evaluation had been scheduled at the jail but had to be moved to University Hospital.

The psychiatrist, Christine Connors, specialized in post-traumatic stress disorder in veterans. She sat down across from him and placed several documents on the desk between them.

"So don't sugarcoat it," Brigham said. "What do you think?"

"Well, the problem with any diminished capacity type of defense is that I wasn't there. Any interview with a mental health expert is almost always so far after the fact that it's irrelevant, because we need to determine her mental state at the time of the crime. But given certain descriptions, I don't think she understood the nature of her crime. She had a temporary psychotic break. I don't think she was fully aware of what she was doing when she killed Mr. Moore."

"There's always a 'but,' I'm guessing."

"But she immediately surrendered and didn't try to shoot herself or any of the officers, which suggests she was consciously aware of the nature of her actions."

Brigham swiveled his chair a little and saw Dr. Connors's eyes drift down to it, so he stopped. Perhaps it looked unprofessional given how serious this case was. "So what are you going to testify to?"

"As a whole, I think she lacked the capacity to conform her conduct to the requirements of the law. But there is some evidence to the contrary, which I will have to reveal to the jury."

He nodded. "And the evidence is that she didn't shoot anybody else or do anything crazy."

"Essentially, yes. I'll write up a full report for you."

He tapped his fingers against the desk.

"This is your first mental health defense case, isn't it, Brigham?"

"How can you tell?"

"Because you sound hopeful. After you've done this for a while, you'll see that it's almost impossible to win on a mental health defense. Even if the defendant has a major psychiatric disorder at the time."

Brigham rubbed the bridge of his nose. He'd had a headache since the previous night that the ibuprofen wasn't touching.

"I'll send you a subpoena for the day of trial. The county'll cut you a check after you testify."

She nodded and left his office.

Brigham leaned back in his chair and closed his eyes. The headache grew in intensity until he could feel the throbbing, as though someone was tapping his head every half a second. He heard something that he thought was part of the headache, but was too loud. It was coming from outside.

He looked out the window to see a car screeching to a halt. Tommy was thrown out, bloody and bruised. He turned around, swearing in Russian, and managed to deck the guy sitting in the backseat who'd thrown him.

Tommy faced the men in the car as they stared back at him for a moment before driving away. Brigham ran out of the office just as Tommy was sitting down in front and wiping the blood from his lips.

"You okay? What the hell happened?"

"It was nothin'," Tommy said, out of breath. "Just a little . . . disagreement was all."

"Who were those guys?"

He took a moment to breathe and then shook his head. "Nothin' you need to worry yourself about. Me and those gentlemen go way back. To the old country." He looked up at him, one of his eyes swelling shut. "How's the murder case going?"

Brigham stared at him. "Tommy, you need a hospital."

He waved him off and rose. "For a few bumps? I'm fine. So how's it going?"

"We have an expert. I think we're as ready as we'll ever be for trial."

He nodded. "Good. Good. I'll be there with you sometimes and I told Molly to go, too. You'll do fine." He put his hand on Brigham's shoulder. "You'll do fine."

Tommy limped away into the office, leaving Brigham staring at his back. Through the window, he saw Scotty watching everything through his thick glasses. Scotty began to twitch again and then turned away from the window.

Twenty-two

Brigham eventually settled his DUI case with one court appearance. The prosecutor was a slim man with red hair who was playing Angry Birds on his phone while they negotiated. The prosecutor agreed to let them plead to a reduced impaired driving charge instead of a misdemeanor DUI, with just a fine and alcohol treatment and counseling.

But when Brigham walked out of the courtroom to inform his client he'd worked out a deal, he could smell the alcohol on her from across the courthouse. She was attractive and middle-aged, wearing a skintight red dress. Even as she stood there, her body swayed in a circle.

"Tanya, are you drunk?" he whispered.

"No . . . no. Are you?"

"You are, aren't you? I can't believe you did that."

"I had a little with breakfast. No big deal."

Brigham glanced back at the courtroom to make sure no one could hear. "The judge will take you into custody if she thinks you're drunk. Look, just stay here. Lemme see if I can get it continued. You can't take a deal if you're impaired."

He casually strolled back into the courtroom like nothing was wrong and bent down near where the prosecutor was sitting. "You mind if we continue this?"

"Why?"

"Just want some more time."

He shrugged. "I don't care. Just clear it with the judge."

Brigham stood and buttoned the top button on his suit coat. He went out and took Tanya's arm, and let her lean against him as he sauntered back inside. He waited with her in the back of the courtroom while the other attorneys called their cases. When they were finishing up, he slowly helped her to the podium.

"Morning, Your Honor."

The judge, an overweight woman with rosy cheeks, eyed him. Tanya's arm was wrapped around his waist.

"The matter of Tanya Dreschel, Your Honor."

She paused and then pulled out the file. "What are we doing today, Counsel?"

"Just a continuance, Your Honor. Two weeks should be plenty of time."

"Does the City stipulate?"

"Sure," the prosecutor said.

Tanya nearly toppled over and Brigham had to pull her body against his. He put his arm around her shoulders and the judge stared at him, then shook her head. "Fine, two weeks."

He turned around and put his arm under hers as he led her out of the courtroom. When they were outside of the building, he took out his phone and called a cab.

"I can drive," she said, her speech slurred.

"You're not driving anywhere. I'll stay with you until the cab gets here. Gimme your keys."

The cab was there in less than five minutes. As they waited, Tanya spoke of her ex-husband and her new boyfriend, who she'd met on a dating website. Brigham helped her into the cab and gave the cabbie her address. He would call her tomorrow to arrange picking up her car. The key was for a BMW.

The car was black with silver rims. Brigham couldn't just drive it straight to the office. He had to go up to the law school and do a few laps before coming back down into the city.

When he got to the office, Scotty came scuffling out, adjusting his glasses.

"Don't tell me you bought that."

"No, it's one of our clients'. She showed up drunk to court."

"Oh," he said, turning around and heading back in. "That happens."

<hr />

In a three-day period, Brigham read two books on cross-examination and trial preparation for felonies. With his DUI continued, he didn't have much else to do anyway.

The theories and techniques nearly contradicted each other. He went online and discovered that there were as many theories on how to successfully conduct a cross-examination as there were lawyers. The one thing they agreed on, though, was that he should never ask a question he didn't know the answer to.

At midnight, two days before the trial, Brigham sat alone in Molly's living room. She was asleep in the bedroom and the television was on, turned low. Brigham stared out the windows at the city. A light rain soaked the asphalt below. There were a few homeless men on the corner, splitting a bottle of beer and laughing. They were getting wet, but didn't appear to care.

"You okay?"

Brigham didn't turn around to look at Molly. "Fine."

"Come to bed."

"I will."

She appeared next to him and put her hands on his shoulders as the two of them took in the city. It had grown, even in just the short time Brigham had been there. It would become like every other major city soon enough: faceless. A place where people got lost and never found themselves again.

"I miss the country sometimes," he said. "Life's a lot simpler in a town of nine hundred."

"Everywhere has its pros and cons."

He turned and looked at her. "I'm going to visit her tomorrow again. What am I going to say, Molly?"

"Tell her the truth. That you don't know how this will play out. You should probably see Vince again, too."

"Why?"

"Prosecutors sometimes change their offers on major felonies right before trial. It's not a fun experience for them, either."

She kissed his cheek and went back into the bedroom. Brigham watched her. Then he turned back around, fixing his eyes on the street corner below. The homeless men were gone.

Twenty-three

The jail floors had been freshly mopped and Brigham nearly slipped in the corridor. He was wearing a different suit, a secondhand one he'd bought specifically for the trial, and had splurged on some wing-tips while at the store.

Amanda's bandages had been removed. She had a scar on her neck. Brigham tried not to look as he sat down across from her.

They caught each other's eyes. Brigham couldn't help but give her a melancholy smile to let her know that he felt the pain she was feeling. She smiled back, an identical smile, and neither of them spoke for a long time.

"How are you holding up?" he said.

"I'll be okay."

"I'm going to have you testify. I don't want to run through your testimony or prepare you. I want everything you say to come from the heart. Juries can see through preparation."

"I understand."

He looked at her hair. It had lost some of its color and appeared greasy. The roots were now a dark black. "Do you need anything?"

She swallowed. "Thank you for helping me. Even if we lose . . . I don't know. I can just tell you care and it helps me."

He nodded. "I bought a dress for you. Well, a woman at our office bought a dress for you, so you look good in front of the jury. We'll have that and some makeup at court tomorrow."

She licked her lips, which were dry and cracking. "Can I ask a favor of you?"

"Of course."

"They cleaned out my apartment. They put everything in a storage shed. Can you get something for me from there?"

"Sure. What is it?"

"A photo. It's of my daughter on her first day of school. She has a . . . a backpack and is smiling. Can you bring that to court for me tomorrow?"

He didn't answer for a moment. "I will."

She nodded slightly and rose. The guard slid the steel door open and she disappeared through it. Brigham stood up and waited until the door slid closed again before turning around and leaving.

The district attorney's office was far from the jail—not even in the same city. Brigham wondered if prosecutors found it uncomfortable to actually see where they were sending people. It reminded him of something he'd read once about the Vietnam War. The ratio of rounds fired to enemy kills was the lowest of any war in American history. The soldiers knew the Vietcong were their enemy, but didn't want to see what killing their enemy looked like. Deep down, even though reason told them what they had to do, it didn't sit well with them.

Brigham went up to the sixth floor and waited to see Vince Dale. Fifteen minutes turned into half an hour, which turned into an hour. The secretary would apologize and tell him Vince would be right out, that he was in a meeting, or a phone consult with a detective, or screening a case that "just couldn't wait." It was a good hour and a half before Vince beeped his secretary and said he was ready. Just long enough to aggravate Brigham, but not long enough that he would leave. Brigham got the impression that Vince Dale knew what he was doing.

Vince's office was as clean as Brigham remembered. Another man sat next to Vince with his legs crossed. He had a legal pad on his lap and a pen in his hand that he tapped lightly against his shoe.

"Mr. Theodore," Vince said. "So glad you called. Please, have a seat."

Brigham sat. "I want you to offer manslaughter, Mr. Dale. Not because I don't want to do the trial or because I'm lazy, but because it's the just thing to do."

Vince smiled widely. "You sound an awful lot like a law school ethics instructor. You know why lawyers become professors, Mr. Theodore? It's because they can't hack it in the law. They can't handle everything being gray and subjective. There are no right answers out in the real world and yet we have to choose an answer anyway. Some people can't handle that. Sounds like you're headed down that path."

"When did it happen?"

Vince glanced to the man next to him with a grin. "When did what happen?"

"When did you lose your soul?"

The comment shouldn't have bothered Vince Dale. But Brigham saw the flush in his cheeks and the moment—just a moment—when he fidgeted and didn't know what to do with his hands.

"Don't get sassy with me, you little prick. I'll bury you."

Brigham didn't respond. Instead, he looked over to the other man, whose eyes were darting between the two of them. "If I beat you in this trial, the news will interview me. I'll make sure everyone knows it's my first case as a lawyer. *Rookie takes down the great Vince Dale, the next DA.* Isn't that election coming up, Vinnie?"

Vince's countenance changed like a shadow had come over him. His cheek muscles tensed. "Get the hell outta my office."

Brigham rose and began walking out.

"And Mr. Theodore. I'll be there when they stick that needle in her arm. Just so you know."

"You do what you want. It's not my place to judge you. God will judge you, Mr. Dale."

Brigham left the DA's office. On the elevator, he took off his suit coat, revealing the wet sweat marks that were expanding across his chest. He mopped his forehead with the back of his hand. As he stepped off the elevators, he saw two detectives heading up. He recognized one of them as the lead detective in Amanda's case. Brigham nodded to him, but the detective averted his eyes and got into the elevator.

As the elevator doors closed, the detective said, "I'm sorry about your client."

Brigham stood there a moment. "Me too," he whispered.

Twenty-four

The night of the trial, Brigham wanted to be alone, so he slept in his apartment. The couple next door fought the entire night. Something about spending money on an item for the house that shouldn't have been spent. Plates were broken, a hole was punched in the wall, and more than once both of them threatened to kill themselves.

By six in the morning, Brigham figured he had been woken at least a dozen times. Groggy, he got up and showered. There was no food in his apartment, so he went out to an Einstein Bagels, got an orange juice and a bagel with cream cheese, and ate alone.

When he arrived at the courthouse, reporters were lined up outside. He'd seen a few of them there for the preliminary hearing, but none of them wanted to talk to him. As Brigham made his way up the courthouse steps, he could see the reporters were huddled around Vince Dale and two other assistants or attorneys. Vince was telling them about the roles of justice and the wave of crime sweeping through the county. He was painting a picture of a massive problem, and of course he was the solution.

Brigham got to the top step before a man stopped him. He was dressed in a blue jacket and wore glasses that were tilted to the side.

"You're the attorney for Ms. Pierce, right?"

"Yes, sir."

"I'm with KSL. I wanted to see if you'd answer some questions."

"Sure."

The man hit a button on a digital recorder. "How did you have a capital case fall into your lap as your first case?"

"How'd you know this was my first case?"

"You passed the Utah Bar exam just recently."

"Oh," he said, glancing back to Vince, who had apparently just said something funny, "that's right. Public information. Yes, it is the first felony I'm trying by myself. I've discussed that with Ms. Pierce and she understands that."

"Don't you think it'd be wiser to step aside and let an attorney with more experience handle the case?"

"No, no I don't. Look, I better get inside."

"One more question. How do you intend to defend a case where five people saw your client commit the crime?"

"Magic. Excuse me."

As he got to the metal detectors, he immediately felt foolish. That had been handled poorly, but the tone the reporter had taken was obviously critical. It didn't sound like that was the tone being taken with Vince.

The bailiff asked him to step out of line and scanned him with the wand. Brigham did his spin and then headed to the elevator.

Judge Ganche wasn't out yet, and the clerks and bailiffs in the courtroom were speaking in hushed tones. They quieted down when Brigham walked in. He took his seat at the defendant's table and the door to the holding cells opened. Amanda came out in an orange jumpsuit.

"Where's her dress?"

"What dress?" the bailiff said.

"The dress I left here two days ago for her."

"Hold on, I'll check."

The bailiff went in back. He came out five minutes later and said, "Sorry, nothin' back there."

"Damn it," Brigham mumbled. He pulled out his cell phone and dialed Molly.

"Hey, I'm almost there," she answered.

"I need you to bring one of your dresses down here for Amanda."

"What happened to the one I bought her?"

"They lost it."

"All right. Be right there."

Brigham sat down next to Amanda and whispered, "Don't worry. She's bringing a new one."

"It's fine, I can just wear this."

"The jury will have already convicted you in their minds. It separates you from them. They'll see you as an outsider. It's important that you look like they do."

Vince Dale finally made his way into the courtroom. A few reporters took spots in the back as he took a tissue and cleaned some dust off the prosecution table. His two assistants set up two laptops and stacks of files. They pulled out obscure legal treatises and stacked them on the table: props for the benefit of the jury.

As they waited for the judge to come out, Brigham thought of the conversation he had had with Tommy last night. With his alligator-skin cowboy boots up on his desk, Tommy took drags from a cigar and said, "Remember that words are just words. Images are what move a jury. And the most powerful are the ones they think up themselves."

Brigham had turned that over and over in his mind all night as he listened to the couple scream at each other next door.

The judge came out just as Molly ran into the courtroom with a black dress. The bailiff took Amanda back to change as the judge turned on his computer and flipped through a few documents.

"No cameras, gentlemen," he said without looking up.

117

The two reporters in the room whispered to their cameramen, who went outside as the reporters pulled out spiral notebooks and pens instead.

Judge Ganche looked at the two attorneys. "Counsel, any chance this is resolving today?"

"No, Your Honor," Brigham said, rising to address him.

Another long silence descended before the bailiff brought Amanda out. She'd applied some makeup and her hair was pulled back with a clip.

The judge watched her hobble across the courtroom and sit down before he addressed her. "Ms. Pierce, do you understand that you are forgoing any plea options and moving forward with a jury trial today?"

"I do."

The judge nodded. "Okay. Well, let's bring the panel out."

The bailiff bellowed, "All rise for the jury."

A jury panel of thirty people filed out of the back of the courtroom. The lawyers turned around as the panel was placed in the audience seating. Sheets of paper were handed out with each juror's name and where they were sitting. Brigham glanced through the names quickly.

"Ladies and gentlemen," the judge began, "thank you for joining us today. You have been impaneled . . ."

The judge spoke for nearly half an hour. He went over the criminal justice process, what they would be doing that day, the type of case they would be hearing, when they would be taking breaks, and then had the lawyers introduce themselves and ask if anyone on the panel knew them.

The jury selection process, known as *voir dire*, was the aspect of trial that attorneys hated the most. It could take more than two days, especially on civil cases where millions of dollars were at stake, and at the end of it, it proved nothing. Human beings were unpredictable. All the research Brigham had done showed him that you could not predict how someone would view new information based on old information about that person.

"Counsel will now begin with their voir dire. Mr. Theodore," the judge said.

"No questions for the panel, Your Honor."

Vince and the judge stared at him. The courtroom was quiet for a moment. The judge finally said, "Counsel, approach."

Brigham hiked to the judge and waited for Vince. He leaned against the judge's bench. Both men were staring at him like he was a child about to be scolded.

"Mr. Theodore, I know you haven't done many of these, but it's customary to thoroughly question the panel. You may have someone on there you don't wish to have."

"I understand, Judge. But I don't have any questions for them."

"All right, well, Mr. Dale, I assume you do?"

"Yes, Your Honor."

"Proceed."

Brigham sat down and watched as Vince spoke to the panel. He began asking them about their criminal convictions, about how many of them had been through the legal system, family members, their favorite TV shows.

"What just happened?" Amanda whispered.

"I don't want to ask them questions. Five people saw you commit this crime, Amanda. If you want an unpredictable verdict, you need an unpredictable jury. I want as little known about them as possible."

Vince joked and laughed and talked about the criminal process. He was using this time with the jury to get them to like him rather than find out anything about them. But once that was established, he began grilling them about every minute area of their lives. He even asked whether any of the jury panel had ever had any sexually transmitted diseases.

Another forty-five minutes passed. By the time the panel was finished with the questions, they looked like they'd been through a polygraph test. Brigham studied their faces. One of the older women smiled at him, a man in a Levi's jacket gave him a dirty look, and another man with dreadlocks looked like he was high. None of which, Brigham guessed, said anything about how they would find on this case.

When Vince was done with his questions, another sheet of paper was passed back and forth between Vince and Brigham. It had the jurors' names on it with a space next to the names. Each attorney was to consider if each particular juror should be stricken for cause, meaning they were unfit to be on the jury. Brigham passed the sheet back without writing anything. Vince struck six people. Brigham didn't object. Then they each had four peremptory challenges, where they could strike whatever jurors they wanted. Again, Brigham left it blank. The jury was chosen after the people Vince struck were excluded. There were twelve jurors on a capital case. Six women and six men, mostly white.

The judge then called a ten-minute break before opening statements. Brigham went out into the hall with Molly. Scotty was there too, shuffling around the halls and peeking into the various courtrooms. He came back to where Brigham was sitting and said, "Vince looks really confident. I wouldn't want to go up against him."

"Thanks, Scotty."

Molly rubbed Brigham's back as he stared at the jurors filing in and out. The attorneys weren't allowed to speak to them. Even a casual comment could result in a mistrial.

Vince came out, too. He gave a few statements to the reporters hanging around and then made a call. He winked at Brigham before going back into the courtroom.

"You okay?" Molly asked.

He took a deep breath and let it out through his nose. "Not really."

"You'll be fine. Tommy wouldn't give this to you if he didn't trust you."

When they went back into the courtroom, the judge was already seated. He was leaning back and staring at the ceiling as though he had been waiting hours. Brigham realized Amanda hadn't been allowed to move.

The attorneys took their seats facing the judge, and the twelve jurors took their seats in the jury box. Brigham's hands were trembling so badly he had to force them under the table.

"Mr. Dale," the judge said, "all yours."

"Thank you, Your Honor," he said, standing and facing the jury. "And thank you, ladies and gentlemen of the jury, for your service here today. And make no mistake, this is a service." Vince paced in front of the jury and then planted himself near the box, one hand placed on the wooden banister. "On July twelfth of this year, a Friday, Amanda Pierce woke up, she had breakfast, she took a shower, and then took a forty-caliber Smith & Wesson pistol out of a gun safe in her home. She got into her car and drove down behind the courthouse—this very courthouse that you're sitting in now. A man was being escorted down the stairs. Ms. Pierce lifted her weapon, and pulled that trigger seven times." Vince stopped and one of his assistants put up an enlarged autopsy photo of Tyler Moore on plasterboard. It must've been taken right after the autopsy, because he was pure white with blue holes in his head, neck, and chest. "She could have shot and killed two innocent sheriff's deputies, she could have killed any number of innocent bystanders, but she didn't care. She wanted to kill this man so badly that she just didn't care if anyone else got hurt."

A long pause.

"I'm not going to stand here and tell you that Tyler Moore was a good man. He was facing charges for the murder of Tabitha Pierce, the defendant's daughter. Did he actually commit the crime? Well, he wasn't convicted because"—Vince pointed to Amanda and stepped closer to the defense table—"she didn't give him his day in court. She didn't allow it. She was judge, jury, and executioner. And no one else was allowed to have a say."

Vince paused and looked each member of the jury in the face.

"You will hear from five witnesses who will tell you they saw the defendant shoot and kill Mr. Moore. Five witnesses. I understand that some of you might be thinking, 'well, vigilante justice is still justice.' Is it? For those of you thinking that, I ask you this question . . . What if Tyler Moore was innocent?"

Another long pause.

"The evidence in this case is irrefutable. The defense will play games and try to find excuses. They may even come right out and try to justify murder. But there is no justification. Amanda Pierce took the law into her own hands, and killed a man. When you go back to that jury room, you must find her guilty. You tell her that she is not allowed to kill whenever she feels like it." He stepped close to the jury box and slapped both hands on the banister, leaning over the jury. "You tell her that murder is wrong."

Vince took a few moments before he sat back down. Brigham sat still. He didn't move even a muscle. Every part of him felt as if it was frozen in a block of ice. Amanda reached over and lightly touched his hand. He turned and faced her. Their eyes held for a moment before he rose. He reached behind him to the few things he'd had Scotty bring to court, and lifted a large photo of his own, three feet by four feet.

Brigham walked over to the photo of Tyler Moore and placed his photo over it. It was of Tabitha Pierce on her first day of school, the same photo he had gotten for Amanda out of storage.

"This is Tabitha Pierce," he said. "Her favorite show was *Sesame Street*, and her favorite food was pizza. But not with pepperoni, because she thought pepperoni made you fart."

The jury laughed. Even the judge smirked. Vince held a cold, steely gaze on him. Brigham knew he wanted to object, but objecting during his opening statement while he was talking about a young girl might alienate the jury.

"She was supposed to start first grade in August of this year. She never got to. Tyler Moore didn't just kill her. In the back of his filthy van, for three hours, he . . ."

Brigham stopped. He looked to her photograph and didn't move. Ten seconds went by in silence. No one spoke, coughed, or cleared their throat. Twenty seconds went by. No one said anything. Finally, Brigham looked up at the jury. He wanted them to picture it. He wanted them to paint the canvas, not him. And they had painted.

Two men were crying. They held it back as well as they could, but the tears were rolling down their cheeks. Brigham had thought perhaps the women would cry first, but maybe the two men, one Hispanic and the other, the white guy with the Levi's jacket, had daughters the same age as Tabitha. Something Vince, in his joking around with the jury, hadn't asked.

Brigham let a good half minute go by in silence before he said, "Her mother sat in a cold police interrogation room as the detective read her Tyler Moore's confession. All the things he'd done to this beautiful . . ."

He stopped. Completely unintentionally, emotion was now choking him. He took a moment before he looked up to the jury. "The prosecution told you that it's wrong to murder. But they're asking you to murder my client. This isn't justice."

Brigham sat down. Another person on the jury was wiping tears away as she stared at the photo of Tabitha. Vince said, loudly enough for Brigham to hear, "Get that down."

His assistant jumped up and took down both photos and placed them where the jury couldn't see them. The judge cleared his throat and said, "First witness, Mr. Dale."

Twenty-five

The first witness in the case was Detective Steve Pregman. He was an older man, skinny with hair that was almost an afro. He was sitting at the prosecution table when he rose and walked to the witness stand. The clerk made him raise his right hand and swear the oath that he would tell the truth, the whole truth, and nothing but the truth. He said he would, and then lowered his hand and took a sip of water.

Vince ambled up to the podium. He leaned one hand against it and said, "State and spell your name, please."

"Steven H. Pregman. That's P-R-E-G-M-A-N."

"And what do you do, Mr. Pregman?"

"I'm a homicide detective with the Salt Lake City Police Department."

Brigham noticed that when Pregman spoke, he always looked at the jury—not the judge or Vince. His back was straight and he wore a suit that was impeccably clean: a professional witness for the prosecution.

"Tell us a little about your training and experience for that position, if you would."

"I've been a police officer for fourteen years, and before that I was in the military. I joined the homicide unit four years ago."

"Do you remember what happened in relation to this case on July the twelfth?"

"Yes, I do. I was doing some follow-up investigation for another case when I got a call from Detective Robert Jones. He said there had been a homicide at the Matheson Courthouse and that the suspect was being held by the bailiffs there. So I met Detective Jones here and we went up to the holding cell where they were keeping the suspect."

"Who was that suspect?"

"Amanda Pierce."

"Identify her for the jury, please."

"She's sitting at the defense table in the dress."

Vince leaned against the podium. "So what happened next?"

"I sat down with her and turned on my digital recorder. I read her her Miranda rights and asked if she would speak with me. She didn't respond, so I asked her about this incident."

"And what'd she do when you asked her?"

"She started crying."

"Did she speak to you at any point?"

"No, she was just crying."

"So what did you do, Detective?"

"After about five minutes, I knew I wouldn't be getting anything out of her, so I ended the interview. I stationed a unit to stay by her while I went out to the courthouse steps in the back. The Crime Scene Unit was already there processing the scene. They had a body, a forty-two-year-old Caucasian male. He was identified as Tyler J. Moore."

"What did you think had happened to Mr. Moore?"

"Well, he suffered from several gunshot wounds to the neck and head. Blood at the scene was consistent with that. I spoke to five witnesses." The detective looked at a notepad he'd brought up with him.

He read the names of five men. "They were all in the vicinity when this incident occurred."

"And what did they say happened?"

"They all said the same thing. Mr. Moore was coming down the stairs, and they saw the defendant, Amanda Pierce, approach him from the sidewalk. She moved up a few steps, turned, and fired several rounds. We recovered seven rounds total, five of which struck Mr. Moore."

"Was anybody else hurt?"

"No."

"Well, thank goodness for that," Vince said, glancing to the jury. "No children were nearby, I hope?"

"No, none that we saw."

Vince nodded. "Now at some point, you tried to talk to Ms. Pierce again, didn't you?"

"After the scene was processed and the Coroner's Office removed the body, yes, I tried talking with her again. We transported her down to the station. I again read her Miranda because I felt that enough time had elapsed, and I asked her to speak with me."

"Did she?"

"No, sir. She didn't speak with me at that time."

"Did you ever determine why she killed this man?"

"Mr. Moore was responsible for the death of Ms. Pierce's daughter. He was facing trial for it."

"Revenge killing."

Brigham shot to his feet. "Objection, Your Honor."

"Sustained. Keep it relevant, Mr. Dale."

Vince smiled widely. "Of course, Your Honor. Thank you." He looked to the detective. "That's all I had, Detective. Thank you for your time."

Brigham took a sip of water. His throat was so dry it ached and felt swollen. He stood up and moved to the podium.

"When you first saw her in that room, Detective, how did she look to you?"

"Look as in . . . her appearance?"

"Yes."

He shrugged. "She looked pale. Shaken up."

"Were her hands trembling?"

"I think so, yes."

"And she was crying?"

"Yes."

"The entire time?" Brigham said.

"Yes."

"Would you say she was crying uncontrollably?"

The detective thought a moment. "Yes. It didn't seem like she could communicate at the moment."

"Could she say anything? Ask for some water? Ask where she was or what was going to happen?"

"No, I don't think so."

Brigham hesitated. "Do you blame her for what she did, Steve?"

"Objection!" Vince bellowed. "That's completely irrelevant."

The judge was about to speak when the detective quickly said, "No, I don't blame her. How could you blame someone after going through what she went through?"

Vince looked like he was about to throw something at the detective's head.

"Objection sustained. Move on, Mr. Theodore."

"No further questions."

"No redirect, Your Honor," Vince said.

"This witness is excused."

As the detective walked in between the defense and prosecution tables, Vince glaring at him the entire time, the detective gave a slight nod to Brigham, which Brigham returned.

"Next witness," the judge said.

The rest of the morning and well into the afternoon was a technical information dump, like reading the encyclopedia. Vince put the medical examiner on the stand and went through the autopsy. Half the jury looked like they wanted to fall asleep. But it was necessary. The law wasn't a piece of wood to be carved by cutting away pieces. It was a house that you built piece by piece, from the ground up. The foundation had to be laid. Even though it was obvious to everyone in the courtroom that Tyler Moore was dead, the prosecution still had to establish it through the testimony of the ME.

They broke for lunch around 1:30. The jury was excused and they agreed to be back in an hour to continue with the medical examiner's testimony.

"Counsel," the judge said, "I've gone through the jury instructions and they seem pretty run-of-the-mill to me. Any objections to any instructions that weren't covered?"

"No, Your Honor," Vince said.

"No," Brigham said.

He had wanted to include every jury instruction he could think of, but Molly had told him that would confuse the jury. While that may not have been bad for some cases, like complex white-collar fraud where it was better the jury didn't understand exactly what had occurred, this was a simple case, and they needed simple instructions. In the end, the only one Brigham had insisted on said that if the jury didn't want to acquit because they felt like Amanda had done it, but they also didn't want to convict and potentially sentence her to death, they could agree that she committed manslaughter instead of murder. It was called a lesser-included offense instruction.

"All right then," the judge said, "break for lunch. Be back at two thirty, gentlemen."

Brigham watched as the bailiff took Amanda away. He turned to see Molly and Scotty staring at him.

"What?" he said.

"That opening was great work," she said.

"I don't think it's enough." He rubbed his nose, hoping to alleviate, however slightly, the coming headache. "Let's grab something to eat. I'm starving."

Twenty-six

After lunch, the trial resumed. Vince questioned the medical examiner for almost four hours. Charts and graphs and computer printouts were presented. A laptop presentation had a computer-animated re-creation of the shooting, charting the trajectory of each bullet.

By the time the ME was through, the jury looked exhausted and the judge had to stop and ask if they needed anything. No one raised a hand, so the judge said, "It's now six in the evening, I think we're going to have to break today and continue with the defense's cross-examination tomorrow."

"I only have a couple of questions," Brigham said. "I'm happy to do them now so that we don't need to bring Dr. Jacobs back, Your Honor."

"Mr. Dale?"

"That's fine, Your Honor."

Brigham rose. "Dr. Jacobs, did you do the autopsy on Tabitha Pierce as well?"

Vince rose. "Objection. Approach, Your Honor."

The two attorneys went up to the bench. The judge, who also appeared ready for bed, had red-rimmed eyes and his hair looked puffier than it had earlier that morning.

"Tabitha's death was tragic," Vince said, "but is not the subject of this trial. Frankly, I shouldn't have even allowed him to bring it up in opening."

"But you did," Brigham said. "And now I get to talk about it. It's relevant because the only question in this case is what Amanda's mindset was when she pulled that trigger. What happened to her daughter caused that mindset."

The judge thought for a moment. "I'll allow it. But if you veer too far off course, I have to shut you down, Mr. Theodore."

"Understood."

Brigham returned to the podium. "Please answer the question, Doctor. Did you do the autopsy?"

"Yes, I did."

"How did she die?"

The doctor hesitated. "Exsanguination . . . she bled to death."

"Bled to death from what?"

Vince casually got up from his seat again. "Your Honor, I have to renew my objection to this entire line of questioning. What happened has no relevance—"

"How can you say that?" Brigham said, louder than he would've liked. "It's relevant. Her daughter's murder is relevant."

"Your Honor, this is a ridiculous waste of—"

The judge sighed. "Everybody, calm down. Mr. Dale, I think defense counsel is right. It's relevant to her state of mind. If you don't think so, you're free to question that. Now let's get this over."

Brigham turned back to the witness. Anger had flared inside him and he hadn't meant for it to. He hadn't even known it was there. "Bled to death from what?"

"She was . . . cut repeatedly."

"Cut how, Doctor? Please be specific."

"Vaginal walls were cut with a precision instrument. A hunting knife or possibly a scalpel. As was her rectum."

"So in layman's terms, he tried to cut out her genitals, didn't he?"

"That would be my best guess, yes."

"And she was alive during this, correct?"

The doctor glanced to the jury. "Yes. My understanding is that he stated he wanted to hear her screaming."

Amanda's head fell. Her eyes glazed over in a way that indicated she wasn't there anymore. At the same time, Vince jumped up.

"Your Honor! This is far more prejudicial than probative."

"That's enough, Mr. Theodore."

"That's all I had. Thank you."

The judge instructed the jury that they were done for the day but were not to speak to anyone about the case. Vince's assistant leaned over and said to him that they should have the jury sequestered so they couldn't read about the things that had happened to Tabitha online. Vince looked to Brigham. Brigham knew Vince didn't want to be the one to suggest the jury be put up in a cheap motel the four days this trial was scheduled for. He wanted Brigham to do it. But there was no way he was about to. He rose, and waited a few moments to see if Vince would actually have the guts to suggest the jury be locked away from their families.

Vince turned a light pink, glaring at Brigham, but didn't say anything. The bailiff helped Amanda out of the courtroom and Molly and Scotty rose to leave as well.

Brigham winked at Vince and left the courtroom.

Brigham tried to spend the evening preparing his cross-examinations of the witnesses to the shootings, but there was nothing there. Just like with the medical examiner, everything they were going to say was true and accurate. But it didn't matter. He wasn't trying to cast doubt on whether the shooting took place, only what Amanda's mind was like when she did it. He decided he wasn't going to cross any of the witnesses unless they said something truly outrageous. Tommy had told him it was better not to cross at all than to cross and look like an idiot, or worse, bolster the other side's case.

Though it was late, Brigham decided to leave his apartment and go to the office. Molly was there working some divorce cases and he could use her company. And Tommy had a certain way about him that made him feel more comfortable with this whole thing than he should have been.

When he got to the office, he found Tommy there, already drunk. A bottle of scotch was on his desk and he poured a drink for Brigham in a tumbler and pushed it toward him. "Drink." It didn't sound like a request.

The scotch was so strong, Brigham began to cough, amusing Tommy to no end.

"So," he said, pouring them both another drink, "how's the trial going?"

"Terrible. Everything they say is true."

"Don't matter. See, they wanna acquit her. But they need something to tell their relatives. When they go home, if they acquit, their wife or husband is gonna be saying, 'what the hell were you thinking?' And we gotta give that next line that they're gonna give them. We have to give them something that will make their spouse back off. Maybe even understand. That's your job. Give them that."

"Well, hopefully the psychiatrist can do that."

Tommy lifted his glass. "Here's to hopefully."

Twenty-seven

The next day, Brigham got to court early. Molly was in a mediation on a custody case all day, so she wasn't sitting behind him. Scotty had his own things going on as well. The only people there were the reporters.

When the judge finally came out, he didn't waste any time and just said, "First witness, Mr. Dale."

The witnesses were two deputies and three bystanders. Two of them were convicted felons who were going into the courthouse on pending charges. But Brigham didn't bring any of that up. It didn't matter, as far as he was concerned.

He watched Amanda. She had a distant stare, like she wasn't even in the courtroom. It made Brigham think of his father, who had fought in Vietnam before marrying his mother. He'd had that same look, as if he'd lost something that he knew he'd never get back.

The deputies testified first, followed by the three bystanders. Their testimony should have been quick, but Vince took his time, as though savoring the fact that the shooting was played out to the jury five times in a single day.

They took only a half hour for lunch, but Brigham couldn't eat. He went down to the cafeteria of the courthouse and bought some apple juice. He sat alone at a table in the corner and watched people. He didn't even notice when Vince Dale sat down across from him.

"Interesting, isn't it?" Vince said.

Brigham was silent a moment. "What is?"

"The people coming in here. Doctors, politicians, lawyers, priests . . . you'd never even suspect the things they did behind closed doors. And yet, here they are. Having to give their pound of flesh. You never know what people are capable of 'cause they don't show you. They don't show anyone."

"I don't see it that way. I think everyone makes mistakes because we're human. There's no handbook on life. We make blunders along the way."

Vince laughed. "You're an idealist, aren't you?"

Brigham shook his head, staring out the window. "Right now, it's Amanda Pierce sitting in front of a jury for one of her mistakes. But it could just as easily be you."

Vince stopped laughing. "I'm still willing to give you the offer. Call off the jury right now and save your client's life, Counselor. She'll hate you for it now, but thank you later."

"She doesn't deserve to spend her life in prison."

"*Deserve* doesn't have anything to do with this," he said, motioning to the courthouse around them.

"Do you even know what's right anymore, Vince?"

"Up yours, you little shit. I'm trying to do your client a favor."

"You're scared you might lose. The jury was crying in opening and your own detective said he didn't blame her for what she did. And you're not going to execute the mother of a murder victim anyway, so don't bullshit me. If we lose, you'll have a press conference where you'll graciously decline to pursue the death penalty against her, due to her service to the country or something. This is about PR to you . . . But this is her life, Vince. Her *life*."

Vince adjusted his tie, as though he hadn't heard him. He rose. "Have it your way. Helluva gamble to take, though. If you're wrong, and I do pursue the death penalty, she's going to die."

Brigham watched him walk away. A woman was trying to push herself through the door with a baby on her hip and a stroller in front of her. Vince saw her, and continued down the hall without getting the door.

When they got back from lunch, everyone seemed lethargic. The jury was slouching in their seats and even the judge looked like he might pass out. Vince, though, seemed full of energy and smiles. A consummate professional.

Amanda looked worse. She wasn't speaking, wasn't asking questions. She didn't even seem interested in what happened there. Brigham knew now what it looked like when someone gave up, totally and completely.

The fourth witness was a man who looked like he'd just come off a long drinking binge, with torn jeans and a T-shirt. He went through what he had seen, the same thing as all the others, and it took a half hour to get the same testimony. But at the very end, he said something no one else had said.

"She looked like she didn't know where she was."

Vince ignored it and continued with his questioning. When he was done, the judge looked to Brigham. He stood up and walked to the podium.

"What did you mean when you said that she looked like she didn't know where she was?"

"After she shot him, I got a good look at her face. I wasn't that far away. She looked confused, like she'd just woken up from a dream or something."

"Would you say she looked like it had just dawned on her what she had done?"

"I guess so."

"But before that, she didn't appear to know what she was doing?"

"She looked . . . on autopilot, if that makes sense. Like she shot him, and then woke up. That's the best I can explain it."

"Nothing further. Thank you."

The final witness went through the same testimony. When Vince was through with the direct examination, Brigham got up and said, "What did she look like after she had shot the man?"

"What'dya mean?"

"Did she seem happy, elated, sad, confused . . ."

"Confused. Definitely confused."

"Like she'd just woken up from a dream?"

"I guess."

"Thank you. Nothing further."

After that witness, Vince called another detective who had been on the witness list. It was his sixth witness and Brigham guessed he only called him to throw Brigham off, since he'd told everyone he would only be calling five.

The detective was a portly man with a thick mustache who had transported Amanda to jail. He took the stand and went through his qualifications, then talked about what Amanda had looked like that day and how he'd felt about it. Apparently she had remained quiet the entire drive, and this was somehow suspicious.

Brigham watched the jury. One man was actually asleep. His eyes would close for a few seconds and then snap open, then close again. One woman was staring at the reporters. The trial was no longer the center of the jury's attention. The witness was irrelevant—it was the first mistake Brigham had seen Vince make.

The day finished at the same grindingly slow pace. Before leaving the courtroom, Brigham asked Amanda how she was holding up. She looked detached, staring blankly at the table as she nodded and said, "Fine."

"Do you need anything?" he asked.

She shook her head. The bailiff came and got her and took her into the back to change and be transported to the jail.

Brigham sat in the empty courtroom for a while. The space was still and lifeless. A replica of the Constitution hung in a glass case on the wall. It was dusty and appeared like it hadn't been cleaned in a while.

Twenty-eight

As he left the courthouse, Brigham turned on his phone. He'd kept it off because as an intern, he'd once seen a judge take an attorney's phone away when it rang during a trial. The attorney was required to come back the next day, pay a fine, and then retrieve his phone.

He had six missed calls and two messages. The first message was from Molly. When he heard it, he nearly dropped his phone. His knees felt weak and a gnawing sickness gripped his guts. He stood still a moment on the courthouse steps and stared out into the parking lot.

Then, he sprinted for his bike.

He got down to the office in a few minutes. Two fire trucks were there plus an ambulance and several police cruisers. Brigham left his bike on the curb and ran over. A uniformed officer wouldn't let him through. He saw a body on a stretcher, covered with a white sheet.

Molly came up behind him. "I can't believe it," she said.

"What happened?"

"He was just walking out of the office. Two men in a black sedan shot him from the street."

The stretcher was loaded onto the ambulance. The EMT hauling it in from the front lost his grip and it tumbled down about a foot. The sheet slipped off from the top, revealing Tommy's bloated face.

Brigham heard one of the cops behind him say, "Fuck him."

Brigham looked back, giving him a hard stare. He made as if to move over to the cop and Molly placed her hand on Brigham's shoulder. "Let's go," she said softly.

Cahoots Bar, near the courthouse, was a place for lawyers and staff to come and get drunk after work. Occasionally you'd see a judge, but that was rare. News in Salt Lake was intermittently slow and reporters would come there looking for tidbits of stories. The last thing the judges wanted was a reporter snapping a photo of them getting drunk in a seedy bar.

Molly sat across from Brigham at the table. She was nursing a beer and flicking some peanuts from a bowl. The bar encouraged you to throw the peanut shells on the floor.

"I don't understand what happened," Molly said. "Could it be a client?"

Brigham shook his head. "I don't think so."

"What the hell are we gonna do? Am I going to have to be a drone at some firm?"

"We'll figure something out."

She rubbed her face with her hands and inhaled deeply. "He took me in when I needed somewhere else to go. I hope he's found some peace."

Brigham didn't respond. Instead, he took a sip of beer, staring at his reflection in the mirror behind the bar.

⌣

Brigham was restless that night. He tried to watch television but couldn't because the noise aggravated him. He'd gotten used to Molly's nice condo, and being back at his own place was disheartening. But he had sensed that she wanted to be alone right then and had told her that he needed to prepare for the next day. Vince declared he had one more witness, making seven rather than the five he promised at the outset of the trial, and then the prosecution would rest.

Molly had tried to convince Brigham to give the case over to someone else on the public defender contract list, but he refused. This had always been his case. It didn't matter whose letterhead it was on.

Brigham changed into sweats and then lay in his bed. The mattress was lumpy and dipped in spots. He tossed and turned for several hours before getting up and putting on his shoes. He left the apartment and walked through the neighborhood. The streetlights were spaced too far apart, so for long periods, he'd be in complete darkness and he'd look up at the moon.

He passed the cemetery. The stillness of it was disturbing. He looked at the row of houses across the street and wondered who would choose to live across the street from a cemetery.

By the time he got back to his place, it was two in the morning. He lay down and closed his eyes, but sleep just wouldn't come.

In the morning, unfocused and unable to concentrate through sheer exhaustion, he dressed and rode his bike to the courthouse as though nothing in the world was wrong. But he felt out of place, weak, lost.

Vince was already in court, speaking softly with someone in a Crime Scene Unit uniform. The bailiff shouted, "All rise," and the judge came in. He glanced to Brigham.

"I heard, Mr. Theodore. I'm sorry."

"Thank you, Judge."

"Well," he said, with a deep breath, "any outstanding issues?"

"No, Your Honor," Brigham said.

"Nothing, Your Honor."

"Okay, let's bring in the jury."

The jury filed in and took their seats. They looked like they'd just stepped off a cross-country bus trip. Hair styling and makeup had fallen by the wayside. Vince rose and said, "The State calls Bradley Chan to the stand."

Chan sat down and was sworn in. He was a technician with the Crime Scene Unit and had processed the Moore homicide. He went through the blood spatter, gunshot residue on Amanda's hands, and the trajectory of the bullets.

His testimony took three hours. Brigham turned to Amanda. She didn't look well.

"What's wrong?" he whispered.

"Nothing."

"When was the last time you ate?" He got no response. "Amanda, when was the last time you ate?"

"Three days ago."

"Are they not feeding you?" he said, anger rising in his belly.

"No, they are. I'm just not hungry. I'm not anything anymore."

Brigham turned back to Chan and pretended to be paying attention. He wasn't sure what to say to her. He didn't know what to do.

"Mr. Theodore," the judge said, "your witness."

Brigham stood up, asked a few quick questions about how the body had fallen, and then sat back down. Objective experts were not a good place to ask many questions.

"Your Honor, at this time the State rests."

Brigham stared at Vince. He should have had one, maybe even two, state psychiatrists discuss Amanda's state of mind. One of them had interviewed her at the jail. But Vince hadn't called him. Without another psychiatrist to contradict her testimony, the only expert on the mental state of Amanda Pierce on the day of the shooting would be Chris Connors, the expert for the defense.

"Okay, well, Mr. Theodore, why don't you call your first witness, unless you have any motions."

"No motions. My witness said she could be here within half an hour of receiving a call, Your Honor."

"Let's break for an early lunch then, and when we get back we'll start with the defense witnesses."

As Amanda was crossing the courtroom, she toppled over. The jury had already left, but someone gasped. Possibly a clerk. Brigham ran to her and helped her up but the bailiff pushed him away. The other bailiff came over and they helped her out.

"She needs a doctor," Brigham said.

The bailiffs looked at each other like they hadn't thought of it. "We'll call the jail nurse," one of them said.

Brigham looked back to Vince, who shrugged and then headed out of the courtroom. The door to the holding cells slammed shut. Brigham wanted to go back there and smack those bailiffs across the face. The woman was starving, nearly dead, and they didn't even pretend they cared.

He texted Dr. Connors and she said she would be there in thirty minutes.

Brigham left the courtroom and sat outside on a bench for a long time before he decided he wasn't hungry. Instead, he lay down on the bench, and closed his eyes.

Twenty-nine

A flurry of movement woke Brigham up. He realized he had slept through lunch, and Vince and his assistants, the reporters, and a few other deputy district attorneys who wanted to watch the trial were piling into the courtroom.

He rose and rubbed the sleep out of his eyes. His suit looked worn and wrinkled. He ran his fingers along the wrinkles as though it would help, then he went into the courtroom and sat.

Dr. Connors was already there, texting someone on her phone from the audience seats. Amanda was there as well. He checked with the bailiffs and they informed him that the nurse had given her some orange juice to drink and said she was fine.

The judge came stumbling out as though he'd been drinking back in his chambers. Ganche didn't appear to be that kind of man, though. Brigham guessed more than likely he had been sleeping, too.

"All rise for the jury."

Brigham rose, as did Amanda. Brigham watched her as the jury came in. She had completely withdrawn into herself. He would not be surprised if she didn't know where she was or what was going on. He wondered if the bailiffs had actually called a nurse to see her.

Brigham knew he'd be putting her on the stand. He had to. This entire case rested on her shoulders. If the jury sympathized with her enough, they would find a reason to acquit her. But he wasn't sure how she would react. If she went up there like this, like some robot with no emotions, the jury wouldn't connect with her.

"The time is yours, Mr. Theodore," the judge said, leaning back in his seat as though he'd just had Thanksgiving dinner.

Brigham rose. "The defense calls Dr. Christine Connors to the stand."

"Dr. Connors, come forward and be sworn."

Dr. Connors took the stand and folded her glasses. She slipped them into her pocket and looked forward, not at Brigham, but at some invisible point on the wall.

Brigham began with the basics. "Please state your name."

"Christine Sylvie Connors. C-H-R-I-S-T-I-N-E, C-O-N-N-O-R-S."

"And where are you employed, Dr. Connors?"

Vince rose. "Your Honor, the State would stipulate that Dr. Connors is an extremely qualified psychiatrist and can speak to the mental state of the defendant. No need to go through her résumé and waste the jury's time."

Brigham glared at him. No attorney ever stipulated to anything on a capital case. Why would he concede so quickly? Surely there were things in her past he could object to and at least challenge her expertise. Maybe bring up the fact that she was paid by the defense on several . . .

Brigham's mouth nearly dropped open.

He looked to Dr. Connors. His entire defense rested on her, and she'd betrayed him. He had absolutely no doubt that if he were to go forward, she would testify that Amanda Pierce was competent and aware that what she was doing was wrong.

He stared at her, unblinking. She stared right back for a second or two, and then looked away.

"Sidebar, Your Honor," Brigham said.

The two attorneys approached the judge. Judge Ganche pressed a button on his desk that sent static through the speakers again.

"Your Honor," Brigham said, "I would ask for an immediate mistrial."

"On what grounds?"

"On the grounds that the State has tampered with one of the defense witnesses."

Vince exploded, "How dare you, you little shit!"

"Fuck you, Vince," Brigham snapped.

"Gentlemen, stop it this instant, or so help me, I will hold you both in contempt and stick you in a cell." The judge looked from one to the other, making sure they understood. "Mr. Theodore, what proof do you have that the State has tampered with one of your witnesses?"

"Last week, Dr. Connors agreed to testify to her assessment of my client. She said that it was a close call, but she didn't feel that Amanda Pierce could have formed the requisite intent required for this offense, and that the murder of her daughter was so traumatic that it caused a psychotic break. She's now essentially a witness for the State and will testify that she did have the intent. The State has promised her something, probably that they'll make her a permanent State expert if she—"

"Those accusations against me are borderline slanderous, Your Honor. I demand Rule Eleven sanctions against Mr. Theodore and that cesspool he calls a firm, for the—"

"Stop it, both of you. I'm serious." He looked at Brigham. "You don't even know what she's going to testify to. So far we have her name."

"Do an in-camera review. She's completely changed her testimony. She drafted a summary of her testimony for me, which I have in an e-mail. Let's see if she sticks to it."

The judge considered this for a moment. "Fine. Both of you, in my chambers." The judge stopped the static. "Ladies and gentlemen of the jury, an issue has arisen that needs to be addressed in my chambers. We are retiring there for a moment before we continue with the trial. Feel free to stretch your legs, though please don't leave the courtroom. Thank you."

The three men and Dr. Connors slipped out the back door and into Judge Ganche's chambers, where he sat back in his executive chair and put his feet up on a footrest underneath the desk. "Mr. Theodore, let me read her report, please."

Brigham brought it up on his phone and let the judge read. It took him a few minutes, and in that time, there was complete silence in the office. Brigham kept looking over at Vince but he wouldn't meet Brigham's eyes.

"Dr. Connors, please have a seat in front of me," the judge finally said, handing the phone back.

Vince and Brigham remained standing. Vince adjusted his tie and flicked a piece of lint off his suit. He still wouldn't look at Brigham or the judge.

"Dr. Connors, the defense has brought up an issue that I would like to explore just a little further, if that's all right."

"Certainly."

"What, and I'm talking about the ultimate conclusion, will be your testimony here today regarding Amanda Pierce?"

"Well, I will be testifying as to the results of my examination of her along with an analysis of her mental health history."

"Which is?"

"I think she formed the requisite intent to commit murder. I think she knew what she was doing. She planned it ahead of time and followed through. That's not madness, that's forethought."

Brigham shook his head, glaring at Vince.

"Mr. Theodore claims," the judge said, "and your report for him seems to indicate, that a few days ago, you were ready to testify that the defendant lacked the mental capacity to form the requisite intent. Is that true?"

"It is."

"And what exactly changed your mind so quickly?"

"Look, as much as we like to believe it is, psychology and psychiatry are not sciences. They are not derived and verified by empirical observation. They can't be, because we can't see or touch the mind. All we can do is see its effects on the brain. So that's what we have. And how we interpret those effects changes all the time. I simply looked at the evidence, and came to a different conclusion."

"And did anyone promise you anything to reach this different conclusion?"

She hesitated. It wasn't a long hesitation, no more than a second, but it was enough. Everyone in that room knew she had been bought and paid for.

"No. No one has promised me anything. I just looked at it and came to a different conclusion."

The judge nodded. "You're excused and may return to the courtroom, Doctor. Thank you."

When the doctor was gone, Vince said, "So what? So she changed her mind. Happens all the time."

The judge leaned forward on his desk. "Vince, you and I go back a long way. I forgive a lot. But if you bribed a defense witness in one of my trials . . ."

"Please. I don't have to bribe anybody. Five people saw her commit the crime."

The judge and Vince argued a bit. Brigham had to keep his eyes on the floor. He couldn't even look up because he was scared he might deck Vince Dale. In one particularly brutal attack, Vince said, "When you got that DUI, who took care of that for you, huh?"

Brigham stored that one away. Maybe it was enough for an appeal if they lost this thing.

Brigham knew exactly what Dr. Connors had been promised. Being a defense expert didn't bring in a lot of money, as only about ten percent of all private defense-attorney cases went to trial. And public defenders' offices had contracted experts they used for every case. But a prosecutor was a different story. They handled two thousand cases a year each. If even ten percent of those required an expert, the experts who were on the short list that the prosecutors called could make a substantial amount of money, and might even get contracts with the cable news shows as experts in their field.

Finally, the judge held up his hand, indicating he'd had enough.

"Mr. Theodore, up to you. We don't have enough evidence for sanctions or charges, but clearly something happened. If you want a mistrial, you got it."

Brigham bit his lip. He had blurted out "mistrial" without thinking. Amanda was losing her grip on reality. What if she continued to deteriorate? They would lock her up indefinitely in a psychiatric hospital. She could spend the rest of her life locked up without ever having been convicted of a crime.

"No, I'd like to go forward."

"With this expert?"

"Yes."

"All right, it's up to you. Let's head back in."

Once they were back in the courtroom, Brigham watched Amanda while the judge set up. When he was ready, Brigham said, "No further questions for this witness."

Vince, a smirk on his face, stood at the podium and said, "Did you perform an analysis of the defendant, Dr. Connors?"

"Objection, Your Honor," Brigham interrupted. "Beyond the scope of direct. All I got from her was her name."

The judge said, "Unless you want to cross about her name, Mr. Dale, I think we're done."

"Of course, Your Honor. No further questions."

"This witness is excused," the judge said, shooting her a disapproving look. "Next witness."

Brigham turned to Amanda. She was staring at the defense table, running her fingers along a name carved into the top with a pen. "Your Honor, Ms. Pierce will be testifying. May I just have a moment with her, please?"

"Of course. Take a side room."

The attorney/client room was no bigger than a bathroom, just a place attorneys used to answer any questions before defendants entered pleas. The bailiff closed the door behind them and stayed outside.

Brigham pulled out a chair for Amanda at a small circular table in the center of the room and then sat down himself.

"What's going on, Amanda?"

"Nothing."

"Amanda," he said, lifting up her chin so they were looking each other in the eyes, "what's going on?"

She shook her head. "I did it, Brigham. I killed him . . . I deserve what they're going to do to me. I deserve to die."

He didn't speak for a moment. "You do *not* deserve to die. You understand me? You did what anybody would do. You had a human reaction and did a human thing."

Until now, Brigham hadn't put into words exactly what he felt about Amanda's situation. And his gut reaction had always been that it was unjust for her to be punished. But now he knew; she had acted how anybody else would have. Only a hypocritical society would put her to death for something anyone would have done in her place.

"Tabitha's gone," he said softly. "That's not an easy thing to accept. You may not want to go on. It's hard. But you just have to decide that you're gonna make it. That the monster that took her didn't take you, too. You have to make it. Otherwise, he will win."

A single tear ran down her cheek and she wiped it with the back of her hand. They sat in silence for a long time. Brigham didn't even notice he was holding her hand until he was ready to go back into court.

"Are you ready to testify?"

She nodded.

Thirty

Amanda was sworn in. Brigham stood at the podium. He mouthed the words *You'll be okay*.

"Amanda, when was the last time you saw Tabitha?"

Her eyes went wide. She wasn't expecting it so quickly. She took a few moments before she glanced at the jury and then down at the floor.

"The day she passed. I had made her breakfast and dropped her off at school before work. We used to meet after school at the bus stop, and that's where she was walking to when . . . when he took her."

"How did you hear about it?"

"A detective came to the house. He had this, like, *look* on his face. And I just knew." She was quiet a moment. "I just knew."

"What happened then?"

"The detective asked if I could go down to the station to talk to him, so I did. He told me that something had happened to Tabitha, that she had been kidnapped and that someone saw the man who'd done it. They got his license plate and went to his house. And they found her body." Tears welled in her eyes and streamed down her face, but she remained absolutely still otherwise. "They found her body in a garbage bag. He wrapped her in a garbage bag, and was going to put her in a dumpster . . ."

Brigham was quiet for a moment, pretending to scribble something down. He wanted that to sink in with the jury. "After her death, what happened to you?"

"I couldn't do anything. I lost my job. I used all my vacation time and then they said that I needed to come back. As if anyone could come back from something like this."

"Why couldn't you work?"

She placed a hand on the banister, as though using it for support. "I can't think. I take so much medication for anxiety and depression that it clouds my thinking. Sometimes I just lie in bed in the morning when I wake up, and cry. I'll cry for most of the day and then I'll have to take something to try and calm myself down. At night, I can never sleep. I just . . . I just see her. What she went through."

The first sob came like a jolt. Her shoulders slumped forward and she put her hands over her face. "I couldn't save her. Oh, Lord. Lord . . . please, make it stop." She was weeping now and Brigham let her. He bought time by getting some tissues from the clerk's desk and bringing them to her. Then he stood by the jury as though he was one of them.

"Make what stop?" he said softly.

"I couldn't save her. This was my fault . . . I couldn't save her. I just see her crying out for me. She must've been so scared. She was crying out for me and I wasn't there. She was crying for me . . ."

"This is not your fault."

Amanda buried her face in her hands. She sobbed for a long time. Brigham observed the jury. The man in the Levi's jacket had tears in his eyes again.

When Brigham thought it'd been long enough, he said, "Were you ever evaluated by a psychiatrist for this case?"

"Yes."

"And what did she say?"

"Objection!" Vince was on his feet. "This is a ploy to get in Dr. Connors's testimony without having me cross-examine her."

Brigham looked to the judge. "I didn't hear a specific objection, Judge."

"Me neither. Overruled."

The judge glared at Vince as he sat back down, the prosecutor's face red as an apple.

"What did the doctor tell you, Amanda?"

"She said that I'd had a psychotic break, and that I couldn't tell the difference between right and wrong, and that's why I did what I did."

Brigham stepped closer to her. "Do you remember the day you shot Tyler Moore?"

"I remember pieces of it," she said, wiping her eyes with tissues. "I remember getting up and I remember standing in front of my gun safe. And then it was like I was in a movie watching what was happening, you know? I didn't feel like I had control over it."

"So you don't actually remember shooting him?"

"No, not the shooting. I remember before, when I parked and went up to him. And after, when I was holding the gun and the deputies took me down. I remember just being in shock and thinking, 'What did I do?' I don't remember anything else."

"Has any memory come back to you?"

"No. The doctor said that during a psychotic break, the memory part of your brain doesn't work. So you don't remember anything."

Brigham turned back to the jury. "If you could tell this jury anything, Amanda, what would it be?"

Dabbing at her eyes with tissues, she managed to calm herself enough to speak clearly. "I want them to imagine my little girl. I want them to think what the last moments of her life were like . . . what she was thinking. What she felt." She looked up to the ceiling, and the tears began flowing again. She was sobbing uncontrollably.

"And then I want them to imagine being me, and hearing what she went through."

Brigham felt the warmth of tears on his own cheeks. He didn't wipe them away as he sat down at the defense table.

Vince stood up. He buttoned the top button on his suit coat and glided to the podium as though he were skating.

"I'm sorry for your loss," he said. "Now—"

"If you were sorry, you would've met with me."

"Excuse me?"

"I came to your office after Tabitha was killed. I wanted to tell you not to make deals with that monster. Your secretary said you were out, but I heard you in your office. You just didn't want to talk to me."

Vince's face flushed red again, but not from anger. Brigham had to suppress a grin.

"You shot Tyler Moore five times, didn't you?"

"That's what they told me."

"And he wasn't hit in the arm or the legs or the shoulders, was he?"

"No," she said.

"He was hit in the head and in the throat. Vital areas."

"I guess so."

"For some robot on automatic pilot, those seem like pretty specific targets, don't they?"

"I wouldn't know."

"Now, I've gone shooting, Ms. Pierce, my whole life, and I can barely hit the target. How was it you shot Tyler Moore standing between two deputies without getting a scratch on them?"

"I don't know."

"You received marksman training in the army, didn't you?"

"Yes."

"In fact, you were given a commendation for your skills as a marksman."

"Yes."

"You were trained to shoot and to kill."

"I was."

"And that's exactly what you did with Tyler Moore, isn't it? You used your training and you killed the man."

"He wasn't a man."

"Do you even regret it? He had a mother, too. Do you regret taking his life?"

"No!"

The courtroom sat silent. Now it was Vince's turn to let that sit with the jury. He ruffled a few papers and said, "No further questions."

The judge looked to Brigham. He shook his head.

"Does the defense have anything further?"

Brigham rose. "The defense rests, Your Honor."

Thirty-one

Closing arguments was the part of the trial Brigham had always been most nervous about. It was the last thing the jury would hear from either of the attorneys. He had never felt himself to be a charismatic public speaker. Vince, on the other hand, was larger than life—a born politician.

"Ladies and gentlemen," the judge said, "we will now hear closing arguments from the attorneys."

Vince got up. He strolled over to the jury like a teacher about to give a lesson to some confused students.

"This wasn't a mercy killing. This wasn't a psychotic break. This was murder. Plain old murder. For the oldest reason that human beings have been killing each other since the Old Testament: revenge. Amanda Pierce was hurt, she was hurt real bad, and she couldn't live with that hurt. And I don't mean to trivialize it. What happened to her is the worst thing that can happen to any parent." He leaned in close, placing his hands on the banister in front of the jury again. "But it does happen. All the time, to hundreds of parents a year. How many of them go out and murder the men responsible? Not many. The vast majority of them leave it in the hands of the law.

"I, you, Ms. Pierce, we're all part of this society. We've agreed to live in harmony with each other rather than in a state of nature where we're constantly fighting and killing each other over resources. And part of this social contract between us is that we have agreed that the law governs justice, not each individual person—that's what truly separates us from the animals.

"You ever wondered why the West grew in prominence so quickly? Why India and China from fifteen hundred on couldn't even come close to competing with us? It's called the Great Divergence. We suddenly drifted away from the rest of the world, and excelled. Why? Because we established the rule of law. A law based on reason, and logic. And we followed that law. China and India are now catching up because they are trying to institute that rule of law. They saw what it did for us and they want it, too. The entire fabric of civilization is held together by this one principle: we let the law determine justice, not an individual.

"Amanda Pierce threw that principle away when she dressed, got out her gun, got into her car, drove down to the courthouse, and shot Tyler Moore. And she didn't just shoot him from the car, wildly spraying bullets everywhere. She sneaked up, shouted at him, and put five bullets into him, and to hell with the two deputies standing next to the man—two deputies who had families. She wanted revenge, and nothing was going to stop her."

Vince took a step away from the jury.

"I asked you this earlier, and I will ask you this again: what if she was wrong? What if Tyler Moore was innocent? Do you want her out there with a gun shooting at people she thinks have wronged her?" He pointed to the man in the Levi's jacket. "What if next time she thinks it's you?" He pointed to a woman in the front row. "Or you? *That* is exactly why we let the law determine justice: so innocent people don't get killed. Amanda Pierce didn't care about that.

157

Amanda Pierce wanted revenge, and to hell with the rest of us. Well, when you go back into that jury room, you tell her no. You tell her it is not okay for her to have your job, and my job, and the judge's job. We let the rule of law run this country. Not an individual. You tell Amanda Pierce that she does not have the right to kill, any more than that SOB who killed her daughter does. She cannot execute a man and get away with it free and clear. That is not how the law works, and I'm asking you to find her guilty. Not because I want it or you want it, but because the rule of law demands it."

Vince looked each member of the jury in the eyes before sitting down.

Brigham rose. He wanted to button the top button of his suit coat, but it was missing, so he just put his hands behind him and let the coat stay open. He walked to the clerk's desk, to a laptop used by both attorneys, and did a Google search. He flipped the projector on, and an image appeared against the wall from the projector mounted on the ceiling. It was of a nude man with a black hood on, standing on a box.

"You guys remember this photo?" Brigham said. "Abu Ghraib. American soldiers and contractors tortured, raped, and murdered Iraqi prisoners of war, most of them civilians. We had five thousand American deaths and over six hundred thousand Iraqi deaths. Do you even remember why we went in? Weapons of mass destruction? There weren't any. Ties between Al Qaeda and Saddam Hussein? Turns out he hated Al Qaeda and never had anything to do with them." He crossed the well and stood before the jury. "We invaded a country that had never attacked us, to take out a leader that told us, in an interview before we invaded, that he was not our enemy. Is that the rule of law Mr. Dale was talking about?

"How about TARP—the Troubled Assets Relief Program? The bailouts of the biggest banks in the world. It actually failed in the House of Representatives when it was first proposed. Our congressmen didn't feel it was fair that the banks should gamble with our money, and then when they lose, be bailed out with our money, too. But two days later, it was proposed again, and it passed the House. Well, what happened during those two days? The rich and powerful talked to each of the congressmen who voted 'no' and gave them something to say yes. It varied from person to person, but they all received something, even if it was just a threat that at re-election time, the biggest banks in the world would support their opponents. And TARP, something the American people hated, passed. Is that the rule of law Mr. Dale was talking about?"

Brigham approached the jury, but didn't preside over them like Vince. He stood a few paces back and looked them in the eyes.

"There's a dirty little secret to this rule of law that Mr. Dale didn't tell you. If you're rich enough, if you're powerful enough, the rule of law doesn't apply to you." Brigham paced a little, his eyes never leaving theirs. "We all know it to be true, but it's so horrific, so against everything we know and love about our country, that we can't face it. We can't even name it. We sweep it under the rug and pretend everything's okay." He pointed to Amanda, stepping closer to her. "Does anyone have any doubt that if she were a senator's daughter, or the wife of a rich CEO, that she wouldn't be sitting here today? Does a single one of you doubt that?

"We all know it's true, and that's what Mr. Dale doesn't want you to think about when you go back to that jury room. That's what this entire justice system doesn't want you to think about. Because ultimately, you are the deciders. And if you knew the system was rigged from the start, you might actually revolt and not do what people like Mr. Dale want you to do. And what does he want you to do? He wants you to crush Amanda Pierce, because she acted like a human being and did what everyone in this courtroom would have done in her place. But she's not rich. She's not connected. She didn't go to the right schools; she doesn't have wealthy parents. She slaves away in a grocery store, having lost her leg in defense of this system that abuses her and treats her like a parasite. And because of that, she sits here on trial, for something that the leaders of our country do every day. Amanda Pierce had a psychotic break. Even Mr. Dale would concede that if you found she did have that break, you must acquit her. She didn't have the requisite intent to commit this crime."

Brigham placed his hands in his pockets, and, borrowing a trick from Vince, looked each member of the jury in the eyes individually. "Amanda Pierce is you. She's me. She's every person out there that acts like a human being. Don't destroy her because she doesn't have the power to fight back. She deserves to be acquitted of this crime, and I am asking you . . . I'm begging you, not to let her down."

Brigham looked at Vince as he sat down. The two men glared at each other as the judge began explaining to the jury what would happen next.

The next hour and a half was spent on jury instructions. The judge read aloud into the record every single instruction, all sixty-three of them. Brigham watched the jury's faces. None of them were paying attention. Once he had learned about jury instructions in his trial advocacy class, he had a gut feeling that they didn't really matter. It was still comforting to know that the mental health defense instructions had stayed in, though, despite the fact that an expert did not testify about it.

Once the judge was done, he rose and said, "All rise for the jury."

Everybody stood as the twelve men and women shuffled out. None of them looked over to Amanda.

"What now?" she asked.

"Now we wait."

Evening had come by the time Molly and Scotty could make it down to the courthouse. They brought a sandwich and some chips for Brigham. Hunger and fatigue, which he'd fought off for the past three days, gnawed at him now.

"How'd closing go?" Molly asked as they sat outside the courtroom on benches.

"Good, I guess."

Scotty adjusted his glasses and said, "You never know what a jury's going to do."

They hung out and played a trivia app on Molly's phone. Several hours went by and they paced the halls, used the bathroom, and went for a quick walk around the courthouse, to the back steps where everything had started.

As Brigham sat on the steps, Molly stood in front of him. She took his hands in hers and they didn't speak for a long time. Scotty was examining the bullet holes that had been left behind by Amanda's gun, using a little flashlight he had on his keychain for illumination.

"So now that you've had time to think, what're you gonna do?" Brigham said. "Since Tommy's gone?"

She shrugged. "I'll figure it out, I guess."

"No big firm job?"

"No, I'd rather get out of law than do that. I'd consider opening my own practice, if I had a partner."

He smirked. "And who would be foolish enough to start a law practice from scratch when the market is saturated?"

"Someone foolish enough to take a homicide as their first case."

Brigham's cell phone buzzed. It was a text from the clerk, letting him know that the jury had reached a verdict.

Thirty-two

The jury deliberation had lasted from four in the afternoon until eleven. The judge had considered calling it a night, but when he sent the bailiff back to check, the jury said they were close to a verdict and would like more time.

Brigham sat next to Amanda. She had a glazed, despondent look. The judge came in and glanced at both attorneys. He asked the bailiff to call the jury in.

"Will the defendant please rise?" the judge announced.

There was no moment Brigham could think of when he had been more anxious or frightened than right then. He stood with Amanda. She reached out and held his hand and he didn't stop her. The jury filed in and took their seats. None of them were smiling at the defense: a bad sign.

"Ladies and gentlemen of the jury," the judge said solemnly, "it's my understanding that you have reached a verdict in this case. Would the foreman please rise."

The man in the Levi's jacket stood up. "We've reached a verdict, Your Honor," he said in his country twang.

"Please pass it to the bailiff."

The verdict form passed from the foreman to the bailiff and then to the judge. The judge read it and handed it back to the bailiff. There was no expression one way or the other on Ganche's face. He simply leaned back in his seat and said, "What say you in this matter?"

The clerk was handed the verdict form next. She began to read . . .

"We the jury, in the above entitled action, find the defendant, Amanda Evelyn Pierce, not guilty of the crime of aggravated homicide."

Brigham felt his knees buckle. He had to press his hand against the table to hold himself up. Before he could look to Amanda, the clerk kept reading.

"In the lesser included count of manslaughter, we find the defendant, Amanda Evelyn Pierce, guilty."

This time Brigham couldn't hold on. He sat down in his seat as Amanda kept standing. Vince swore under his breath and said something like "Dumb fuckers," before packing up his exhibits and laptop.

The judge excused the jury and thanked them for their time. One man, the man in the Levi's jacket, stared at Amanda, some strong emotion in his eyes, but then he turned and walked out with the rest of them.

The maximum sentence for manslaughter that had been reduced from aggravated homicide was still a first-degree felony, which meant Amanda could get six to life.

Brigham felt weak and dizzy. His hand slipped out of Amanda's. The lesser-included instruction had worked as it should have. It was a compromise between aggravated homicide and an acquittal. But the thought of Amanda spending the rest of her life in prison sickened him so much that he considered quitting right then and there, resigning from the Bar and never setting foot in a courtroom again.

"Mr. Theodore," the judge said, leaning forward, "your client has the right to be sentenced in not less than two nor more than forty days. I suggest you waive minimum time for sentencing and be sentenced today."

Vince looked from Brigham to the judge. "Your Honor, I would like a pre-sentence report prepared. I'd like the family of Mr. Moore to come in here and give their statements to the court. I need time."

"It's not your time to get, it's hers. Ms. Pierce, do you want to wait and give Mr. Dale time to prepare, or do you want to go forward now?"

She peered at Brigham. He nodded.

"I'd like to go forward now."

"Your Honor, I must object again," Vince said, anger rising in his voice. "This is a first-degree felony. I need time to prepare for sentencing."

"Noted. But I'm going forward today. Ms. Pierce, do you have anything to say?"

"No."

"Then I'm proceeding with sentencing at this time. I'm ordering you to three years' supervised probation through Adult Probation and Parole. I order you to complete a psychiatric assessment and provide proof to this court of your ongoing treatment during the length of probation. I am also ordering you to one hundred hours of community service and to pay restitution to the family of Mr. Moore for any burial costs. I am ordering no further violations of law with the exception of minor traffic offenses. That means if you commit another crime, I can sentence you to the maximum of six years to life at the Utah State Prison. Do you understand?"

"Yes," she said.

"Good. I'm ordering your release today. Please set up the supervised probation within forty-eight hours. And Ms. Pierce, good luck to you."

"Thank you, Your Honor."

The bailiff unlocked the cuffs around her wrists. She stared in disbelief and turned to Brigham, who had the same look on his face. She kissed his cheek and wrapped her arms around his neck.

"Thank you," she whispered.

"No . . . thank you."

She pulled away from him, holding onto his hand until the last moment. She disappeared with the bailiff into the back room.

After Amanda and the judge left, Brigham sat on the defense table, staring at Molly, who had the widest smile he'd ever seen.

He looked over when Vince left the courtroom saying, "Enjoy it while it lasts."

When they were alone, Brigham hopped off the table and threw his arms around Molly.

Thirty-three

The office was small and the heating didn't work correctly. The receptionist out front was part-time for now until they could afford a full-time employee. In the back were three offices and a conference room. Scotty's office was already packed with reams of paper, files that he'd been working on and off for the past few years. Molly's was clean, everything in its place. Brigham's was empty except for a desk, chair, and computer.

The offices above them were filled with engineers and the ones below with accountants. They were the only attorneys in the building, and in the three weeks they'd been there, every tenant had come with some sort of legal problem. They'd also gotten several clients who had seen the news coverage of the Amanda Pierce trial.

It was late evening, and Brigham had spent the entire day at a preliminary hearing on a drug case. His muscles felt weak, but his mind was sharp, excited, and on edge.

A bottle of scotch and a tumbler with ice sat on the desk. Brigham poured two fingers, his feet up on the desk as he relaxed back into the leather chair. He raised the glass.

To hopefully.

Acknowledgments

The author gives a big thank-you to Amazon and Thomas & Mercer, my editor Kjersti, and all the criminal defense lawyers slugging it out in the ring every day against monstrous odds and with little thanks.

This book is based on a true story, and I've recalled facts and events as best as I remember them. However, to protect the identities of my clients (and to not have judges and prosecutors throwing things at me for revelations in the book), I've changed names, dates, and locations, and truncated various events to fit the narrative.

If you enjoyed this book, please return to Amazon and leave a review. Reviews not only encourage authors to write more, they improve our writing. Shakespeare rewrote sections of his plays based on audience reaction, and modern authors should take a note from the Bard.

So please leave a review and know that I appreciate each and every one of you!

About the Author

Photo credit: FotoFly Studios 2014

Victor Methos was born in Kabul, Afghanistan, and lived in Pakistan and Iran before permanently settling in the United States. A fluent speaker of several Middle Eastern languages, he studied science, philosophy, and religion at the University of Utah before attending law school. He's worked as a prosecutor specializing in violent crime and is currently a criminal defense attorney. He divides his time between San Diego, Las Vegas, and Salt Lake City.